All The Things I Would Do

GW00391149

Amie Collins

First paperback edition April 2020

ISBN 9798616942784 (paperback)

www.amiecollins.co.uk

For all those who hide

Prologue

Maybe if we stopped caring about what everyone else thought of us we'd be more free in life. Free to do and say as we want without being terrified of the consequences, even when the worst that'll happen is laughter in your face or a few hurtful but meaningless words strung your way. We're all so concerned with what others think of us that we put the opinion of people who mean nothing to us at the same level as those who mean the world. We become so trapped in ourselves that even when we can be who we really are, we've forgotten who that person is. We lose ourselves trying to please the people who do not matter and then we can't find ourselves in time for those who do. And worst of all, you forget who you are and you're forever wondering what really lies beneath the surface.

And we're all too scared to do anything about it.

People always say I'm shy, and it's true; I am shy. But I'm shy because of the fear holding me back. I never answer questions in class or do anything that involves putting myself out there or being noticed at all because I'm always scared that people will judge me or laugh at me. The thought, "What would I be like if I had courage?" swims into my mind, unbidden, when thoughts begin to spiral. Sometimes I wonder if I could be like that, but then, I immediately swat away the stray thought – or at least try to, secretly hoping it won't reappear for years to come. But it always does. In the end.

1

Stepping off the bus, I walked as quickly as I could without looking like I was running away – which was exactly what I was doing. Not that anything had technically happened, but that doesn't mean the stares of those girls behind me weren't distinctly unsettling and uncomfortable, and I wanted to get away promptly.

Even after I'd entered the school building, and weaved through other students, dissolving into the crowd, I didn't slow down. Because even though I was away from one predator, others could still be lurking. I didn't like the corridors, with the too-bright paint and photos of students who had left the school before I'd even started scattered along the walls. I was an easy target for those looking for one, and I wasn't inclined to become such a target. So I kept my head down and walked quickly and tried to ignore the sadness which bloomed within when I heard friends talking, laughing, enjoying themselves in the minutes leading up to the start of the day.

I swallowed down the lump forming in my throat as I walked past an old friend, Jane, who was laughing with her new friend group – the girls who gossiped and cared about their nails more than their grades. She was the only person I'd ever talk to, before she discovered looking pretty was the most important thing for her. She decided I wasn't good enough for her anymore, leaving me stranded on my own. I hadn't gotten another true friend since.

I sped up, shrinking into myself even further.

But I'd barely gotten a few steps when I heard my name, just in front of me. I looked up and tried to hide the wave of feelings flowing within me at the sight of George. His blue eyes shone brightly and his light brown hair – almost blonde – was cut short. I slowed down, almost stopped, but started walking beside him instead.

"Hey, Zoe," George said casually, sweetly. It wasn't unusual for us to talk, we messaged regularly and we were in a few of the same classes. But it still surprised me every time. I know how I must have come across: shy, sad and lonely. And on no world is that desirable.

"Hi," I said, more quietly than I'd have liked. But my voice didn't seem to get any louder than that – it was as if, subconsciously, I was stopping myself from being heard.

"How was your weekend?" George asked, not deterred by my timid nature. He never was. It was like he was determined to bring me out of myself and make me talk to someone for once. I think he knew he was the only person I ever talked to – and even that was hardly ever about anything meaningful – and, being the blessing of a person he was, he made sure I didn't close myself off completely. I didn't deserve to have a friend like him, let alone anything more.

"Oh, it was fine. How was yours?" I said, hoping he didn't notice the nerves laced in my voice. I tried to smile up at him, but I wasn't sure if it even reached my cheeks, let alone my eyes. Normally he could make me smile more, but not today. Somehow the sadness, the worry, the feeling I wasn't good enough, was etched into my being too deep for a simple smile to lessen the pain. But I didn't want him knowing that, so I forced the smile wider, hoping beyond hope it didn't look like a grimace.

"It was good, thanks. I practised a new song on the guitar, but I can't seem to get it right." He said it so easily, so unlike anything I ever said. Like an easy-going nature was his natural state, while an anxious one was mine. I smiled again, hoping again that it somehow put across the idea that I wasn't as much of a wreck as I appeared to be. But who was I kidding?

I was acutely aware of how close our arms were as we walked side by side, in the narrow corridor. Half of me wanted to move closer so they'd brush against each other more, while the other half knew that was too risky and I might show my true feelings. So I stayed where I was, pretending I didn't have butterflies flying around my stomach.

We'd come to his tutor room, and he stopped walking just shy of the door, so I stopped too, in front of him as he turned around to face me.

"So, I'll catch you later?" George asked.

I blinked. And again, fumbling for something to say. "Um, yeah, sure," I mumbled, inwardly cringing. I was overly aware of how stupid I must have seemed, being so shocked and confused at his offhand comment. Who does that? Who is shocked at something as mundane as that?

George started to turn around, saying goodbye over his shoulder, while I stumbled over replying. I stood there for a second, debating whether to say something else, but he'd already half moved towards the door, and I didn't have the guts to call him back, so I took a deep breath and carried on walking to my tutor room, which was the other end of the short corridor.

Sliding into my seat, I wondered why George bothered with me. I was grateful for him, incredibly so, but I was confused, nonetheless. He was nothing but kind to me, while I barely talked and didn't give him half the credit he deserved, or even half the kindness. And I felt so guilty about that. He didn't deserve it. He deserved so much better than me.

But despite the shame and guilt bubbling inside of me, I didn't know if I could change. I didn't think I had the strength to open myself up to him more – or anyone for that matter. I'd been hurt before, and I didn't want to feel that ripping, overpowering heartache that came with betrayal when someone left you again. I didn't want to feel that way, but I couldn't let myself hope for anything better or take the steps to get there. I couldn't. At least, I felt I couldn't.

Though I wished I didn't shy away from every living thing in sight, didn't close myself off. I wished I could feel more confident in my own body and in myself. But a part of me felt I didn't deserve that happiness, while another part was convinced I could never do it.

The other part? That part of me wanted to try it: try opening myself up a little and open my heart to other people, letting people in and giving them the power to hurt me, but trusting that they wouldn't.

2

When I woke up, I stretched for my phone and stared at the screen. Nothing. Again. No messages, no likes, nothing. It's not like I was surprised. Who would message me anyway?

I started getting ready for school in a daze, desperately trying to push all the negative thoughts out of my mind, although only succeeding to a small extent.

First thing in the morning of a school day was always the worst, purely because I thought of all the possible bad things that could happen — most of which never did — partly so that I'd be surprised when something good happened, but partly because I couldn't help it. I couldn't help worrying and agonising over what could happen in the day ahead. I knew I shouldn't do it, I knew it only made it worse, but I did it anyway, ignoring any good sense I might have had. That's what happens when you do something enough; it gets ingrained into the essence of your existence and before you know it, it's too late to change it. Old habits die hard.

As I walked to the bus stop, my thoughts drifted to the whole "being-courageous-thing" and whether I should try it for one day. Just one day. What harm could one day do? It may be a horrible day, but it'll end eventually, and I won't have to do it again. And if it goes well, then that's great, maybe I could try it more often. I glanced down at my timetable, after fishing it out of my pocket, to see that I had English first, which was a pretty good lesson to try and be more active when answering questions.

But, no, I thought. I couldn't try it. I shouldn't have let the thought progress that far. It's not an option; it couldn't be. I never would have been able to do it. I wouldn't be able to keep my hands from shaking or sweat from beading on my forehead. No, I can't do it, I told myself. I shouldn't.

The whole journey to school was quite long, which gave me plenty of time to talk myself out of it.

But, when I stepped off the bus at school, I'd resigned myself to giving the whole "courageous thing" a try. After all, what's the worst thing that could happen? I answer a question; people stare at me; maybe they laugh or maybe they don't. Maybe it'll be unbearable, I thought, but I'll bear it and I'll be fine. I wasn't going to back out now, and I'd make sure I carried on for the entire day, pushing through the discomfort that was sure to arise. But it's just one day. One day. I could do that. I repeated that to myself again and again: a mantra. I'll be fine. It's just one day. I can do this. If you tell yourself something enough times maybe you start to believe it.

But, on the other hand, it might turn out alright. And it was that possibility which kept me going.

I couldn't possibly know how it would work out, but, despite my suffocating fear, I was smart enough to know I needed to at least try. A part of me needed to know what I could do and what I was capable of, and that wasn't going to happen when I was hiding behind a wall, distancing myself from everything around me. A part of me needed to know there was more to myself than the shell of a person I'd become. I needed the confirmation that I wasn't a soul trapped inside a body that I didn't fit in. I needed to prove to myself that maybe I could mould myself to someone I actually liked – or at least didn't hate. I could make my skin fit.

And, even though I had to keep reminding myself of this want, this need, and fight down the overpowering urge to just give up and crawl back inside myself, I knew it was the right thing to do. It had been almost impossible to dismiss the idea for a while, and I think that's because, subconsciously, I knew I needed this. I knew this is what it was going to take to be closer to the person I wanted to be and to even have a slight chance of being better and doing what I really want to do in my life.

And if that means one truly awful day, then so be it.

At least I'll know I tried.

3

I pushed open the door to my tutor room and, after softy clicking it closed behind me, walked to my seat, desperately trying to avoid all the other chairs laid out in front of me as obstacles. Sliding into the chair, I pulled out my history homework from my bag. Tutor didn't start for another fifteen minutes, meaning there were few people in the classroom and the teacher wasn't there yet. Most people tended to talk right up until the last second before Mr Brown stumbled in and commanded us all to be quiet and get on with our work. But I always started doing something as soon as I sat down, in an attempt to seem like I sat on my own for a reason, rather than the harsh reality that I had no one to sit with.

People slowly started to fill the room while I continued with my homework, and I knew I shouldn't have been acting like usual: head down and shoulders slumped to make myself small, in a futile attempt to become invisible. Tutor wasn't the time to be courageous, at least not yet. But when I looked up for the first time since I'd sat down, a couple of minutes before the start of the day, Emily, a girl who always sat in front of me, was just coming through the door. She had dark blond hair, falling just above her shoulders, and she always wore a sweet smile, with kind eyes beneath her deep purple glasses. She always sat on her own, like me, but we normally only ever talked when we were forced to do anything in pairs.

She smiled at me as she came to her desk. I smiled back, and before I could stop myself, said, "Hey, Emily. How're you?"

She seemed momentarily surprised, but recovered quickly and sat down in her chair, swinging her legs over the side to face me. "Hey, Zoe. I'm pretty good, thanks. You?"

We continued to talk, about meaningless things, until Mr Brown came in, slamming the door behind him and making Emily jump. She flashed me an apologetic smile before turning around in her seat to face the front and started doing some work.

I looked down and picked up my pen, but I couldn't focus on the Vietnam War anymore. Warmth was spreading through my body, just because I'd talked to someone and actually enjoyed myself. I wasn't worried she'd judge me, and I felt more like myself than I had in a long time, talking and laughing with Emily. And that was all I needed to give me that extra push and confidence to put myself out there and talk to other people.

Because, really, that was the main problem. I shut myself off from everyone and didn't let anyone in, telling myself it was for the better: that way, I couldn't get hurt. But there's far more to life than simply not getting hurt. There're happiness and friendship, and I'd closed myself off from that. But, sitting in that classroom full of people whispering to their friends despite Mr Brown's

10

piercing stare, I was determined to change that, and let other people in.

After tutor had finished, I smiled at Emily and said goodbye before walking to my English classroom. I made a silent promise to myself to work to form a friendship with her, and not let myself run away from the potential of happiness as I have in the past.

The classroom was already half full by the time I walked in, and I made my way to my seat in the second row. Before I had the chance to unpack my bag, I made eye contact with George, who had just come into the room. Normally I would have looked away quickly and hoped he hadn't noticed me, but not today. I smiled at him brightly from across the room, and I noticed his step falter slightly, before smiling back at me. The smile lit up his face, reaching his sky blue eyes and making his already kind features even kinder. He sat directly behind me and when he got to his seat, I asked how his band practice went that morning – he'd told me a few weeks ago when his band practised and I'd filed the information away.

He, like Emily, was surprised by the fact that I started a conversation – he tended to be the one to speak first – but he seemed happy to talk to me and he had the grace to ignore the shift in our dynamic. I listened to his story about how the strap of Dan's bass broke during practice and he had to sit down for the remainder of the session, and to make things worse, it was out of tune, too, distracting George, and I watched how his mouth curled up into a smile as he told it, and how his eyes shone when he laughed.

I could have listened to him all day, just listening and watching him talk about the thing he loves most, but

Mr Reed was quietening the class and we were forced to stop talking and sit down in our seats. I was half tempted to turn around in my seat to carry on our conversation, but I was being courageous, not rebellious, and I wasn't about to get a detention for the first time in my life.

Mr Reed told us which poem we were going to be looking at and I flicked through my anthology to find it. He gave us some time to look through it and prepare to answer some questions, and I mentally prepared myself to speak in class. I reminded myself that there're technically no wrong answers in English and that my class was relatively nice and wouldn't bite my head off. So, when the teacher posed his question, I tentatively raised my hand into the air and tried to ignore the thirty shocked faces around me. Mr Reed looked slightly confused, blinking, as if he couldn't trust his own eyes. He didn't even bother scanning the class to see who else put their hand up, but called on me quickly, like this might be the only opportunity he'll ever get to hear from me. At the beginning of year ten, when I first had him as a teacher, he'd tried to persuade me to talk in class, but he'd quickly resigned to my silent presence. I wasn't distracting anyone, and I did the work, so he didn't mind.

I could feel thirty pairs of eyes on me as I spoke, but not one of them felt negative. Mr Reed looked so shocked and pleased at the same time that it was almost comical, and I'd left him lost for words, as he cocked his head to the side, looking at me like he couldn't quite figure me out.

After what felt like an eternity, he cleared his throat and said, "That was really good, Zoe, I hadn't even thought of that."

My heart swelled with pride. It could be difficult to please that man.

I answered a couple more questions throughout the lesson, giving my opinion on what I thought the poet was trying to show and what it represented, and each time Mr Reed looked happy with whatever I'd put forward. But, to my utter surprise, it wasn't horrible. It was nice, even. I've always loved English, and it felt freeing to speak all the thoughts I always had regarding the text. I used to scribble down my thoughts in my book, so voicing them too was an odd, but welcome, change. I wondered why I was so worried to do it because there was nothing to be worried about. It was easy.

I had just finished packing up when Mr Reed walked over to my desk and stood in front of me for a moment before speaking. People were starting to file out of the classroom, but George was still behind me, seemingly just standing there, from what I could tell.

"Really well done today, Zoe. It was wonderful to hear your thoughts, rather than reading them in your essays. You had some brilliant things to say, and it was obvious that a few of the students were in awe of what you came up with – I know I certainly was. Keep it up; you did great." He smiled then, adding more meaning and power to his already uplifting words.

I nodded, smiled widely and said, "Thank you, sir. I'll try." A promise to both myself and my teacher.

"Good, I'm glad."

With that, I picked up my bag, smiled again to George and walked out of the classroom, giving my thanks to Mr Reed once again. But before I could get very far to my next lesson, George's voice called my name behind me.

I stopped walking and spun around to face him, smiling at him again.

"Hey, I just wanted to say, well done for that. I know that must have taken some courage to speak up as you did. And, er, I'm proud of you," George said, somewhat sheepishly, which is a lifetime away from what is usual for him. But he was smiling at me, beaming really, which made me smile even more than I already was.

"Thank you, that means a lot," I said. It sounded flimsy and silly, but I didn't know what else to say. There were so many feelings whirling within me.

We'd started walking to our next lesson, maths, which we also had together. "I also wanted to ask, if you wouldn't mind, meeting me at lunch?" He sounded almost worried, like there was a lot hanging on my answer.

I didn't speak for a moment, unsure of what to say. But then I remembered what I'd promised myself: I'd put myself out there, and this was certainly that. Plus, this is what I've wanted for a while now, a chance to spend more time with George. So, before I could change my mind or think of any reason to decline, I said, "Yeah, sure. Where do you want to meet?"

His face obviously lightened at that, and he told me to meet him by the basketball courts at the beginning of lunch. I nodded enthusiastically, and was about to ask him why he wanted to meet, but I realised the class had already gone in, and I didn't want to be late, so we sped up to slide into the classroom before the teacher closed the door, and I missed the opportunity to ask George anything.

Instead, I smiled back at him and nodded, another confirmation that I'd be there. As I sat down, I tried to pretend that I didn't have butterflies in my stomach at the mere thought of time alone with George.

4

The next two lessons seemed to last a lifetime, my heart pounding more and more as the seconds ticked closer to the start of lunch. Jitters ran through my body, and I was apprehensive, but also so excited that it overruled the fear cascading over me.

When we were finally let out of history, I packed up quickly and walked over to the basketball courts where I'd promised I'd meet George. My class had been let out a minute or two late, and George was already standing by the wall of the school by the time I got there, his bag slung over his shoulder and his eyes squinted against the sun. The air was neither warm nor cold, and the sun held only a little heat, as was common for South England in late September.

He looked up just as I was getting close, and the moment he saw me his mouth broke into a wide grin, dispelling any worry which was previously etched into his skin. I couldn't help but smile back, just as widely, at the sight of his adorable grin. It made butterflies flutter in my stomach and made the worry which had been building up – from both this meeting and putting myself out there all day – disperse so suddenly that I questioned its presence in the first place.

"Good afternoon," I said in mock politeness. It was so far away from how I usually acted, how I talked to him, that it shocked me. But I liked it: I liked how bold I was being and I liked how it only made his already wide grin impossibly wider, and he laughed for a moment, before saying the same back to me, with a gentlemanly nod of his head.

I expected him to say something more, maybe about why he'd asked me to meet him when we'd never purposefully met up before – it had always been coincidences or before or after shared lessons – but all he did was cock his head to the side and smile at me.

After a moment, I asked, with a smile in my voice, "What is it?" Normally, I would have been feeling beyond self-conscious, but his warm and gentle gaze only made comfortable warmth spread through my blood, rather than the crawling and itching sensation usually elicited when someone looked at me.

He shook his head a little and laughed. "Nothing. So, shall we walk?"

"Yeah, sure," I replied, slightly confused as to where we'd be walking, but as he headed off toward a cluster of picnic tables it became obvious. I rushed to fill the couple of steps between us so we walked side by side. Neither of us said anything, making for a surprisingly comfortable silence.

"How was history?" George asked, sounded genuinely interested.

"Really good, thanks, we've been looking at the Vietnam War, and it's really interesting. Sad though, but interesting. How was music?" It's funny, we basically knew each other's timetables, even after only a few weeks back after summer. Maybe we'd become closer than I'd realised. It made a glimmer of hope ignite in my heart.

"Good, I finished my composition." We'd just come to the benches, and I sat down, dropping my bag next to me while George sat down opposite and pulled out his lunch. I did the same, grateful to have someone to eat lunch with. I normally ate at the tables, though I was normally alone, with other groups of friends around me. It wasn't great, but it was far better than facing the canteen and trying to find somewhere to sit that didn't involve looking like a loner: an impossible task. It worked for the most part, though when winter rolled in, I'd have to head inside. But I tried not to think about that.

Before I had a chance to say anything, George continued, "So, I was wondering if you'd like to come to band practise after school today? Meet the band and hear what we've been working on?" He sounded so vulnerable, like he was showing me a new and intimate side to himself. Which he was, really. I knew music was such a vital part of his life, so showcasing it would be like showing a part of yourself. That's what it was always like with my artwork, and I couldn't imagine music would be any different.

That's why I was so sorry I had to say no.

I smiled at him, and his face lit up in hope. "I'm really sorry, I'd love to come, but I won't be able to get home if I don't get the bus."

It was almost true. Technically, I could have called my parents and they might have been able to pick me up, but they always hated when plans changed last minute like that, and I didn't want to give them yet another thing to have against me.

For a moment, George's face fell, and the disappointment was so blindly obvious it broke my heart a little to be the one to create it. But he quickly recovered, the pain gone almost as suddenly as it had arrived, and he smiled brightly at me. But I could tell it was only covering up his true feelings.

"Of course, that's ok."

"Another time though, ok?" I suggested, almost weakly. I was hoping for something a bit more promising than a shallow suggestion, but I seemed unable to provide anything better.

"Yeah sure, I'll let you know." But the conviction had left his voice.

We sat in silence for a short time, both of us eating our lunch, then he looked up and smiled at me slightly, a twinkle in his eyes which made my heart flutter inside my chest.

"You're different," George said suddenly, like he wanted to say it before he changed his mind.

I was at a loss for words, and when he noticed that, he scrambled to elaborate. "It's just, you seem so much more involved. You've come out of yourself a bit and you … you're less tense."

My brain was whirring so much that I could barely apprehend what he was saying, let alone fathom a response. He looked like he was expecting something, but he was waiting patiently for me to reply.

"I'm trying something new," I finally said. But George stayed silent, gazing at me from across the wooden picnic table like my words held all he could ever need to hear. But I was sure I was imagining it. I carried on, not caring – or even minding — that I was letting him see a new and vulnerable side of me.

"I had to try to make myself actually do something. I'd gotten too used to making myself invisible and closing myself off from people. It was doing more harm than good. I couldn't live with myself, knowing I never even tried to become something more. Because I know there's more to life than hiding from those who might hurt me and running away from any kindness. There has to be more."

George just looked at me for a moment, an admiring glint in his eyes. He nodded – to me or himself, I couldn't tell – as if in approval. Then, he smiled brightly.

"Well, I like this. You're more yourself than I've ever seen you. And I think you will find that there is more to life than that. Much, much more."

My mouth pulled into a grin that I couldn't dispel even if I wanted to. "I hope you're right."

•••

By the time I got home that afternoon after school, I was almost giddy with the success of the day. And I was determined to keep it up. Because though it was nerve-wracking, I didn't let that stop me from becoming more visible. And it got easier after I realised how simple it was.

I picked up my sketchbook and grabbed my pencils, sitting down at my desk and opening the book at the next empty page. I'd been lost on what to draw for a while, but the pencil flowed easily now, my determination and happiness driving me forward in my art. A face started to appear on the page – not mine, but someone that could be me if you had a good imagination. The girl I'd drawn was smiling, a real smile that reached not just her eyes, but her whole face. And suddenly I knew exactly what I wanted my next project to be. I wanted to show how I didn't need to hide anymore, that I could let other people see me without being terrified. I didn't need to lie or hide my emotions and I didn't need to stay silent. I could continue opening myself up to other people.

As I drew, my desire to carry on only grew. I thought about lunch with George that day and I couldn't help but smile and feel comforted by the thought. And I think it was that that made me really want to continue. Emily also contributed, as did the positive comments from teachers, but it was George who really made the difference, I think. Because I knew I wanted to become closer to George, and for our friendship to progress into something more. And that wasn't going to happen when I was hiding inside myself. And that half-hour spent together, simply talking and laughing and smiling, made me so happy and relaxed that I'd step out of my comfort zone to have that joy more often. I thought about all the things I would do if I put myself out there more, and before I knew it I was fantasising about going to more clubs, making more friends and being more comfortable in my own skin. I could laugh unselfconsciously, talk freely in a group without agonising over what I was saying or simply walk down the halls without fear.

And, though the thought both terrified and excited me, I knew I had to go through with it. I should have stepped out of myself a long time ago, but I owed it to myself to at least start now.

5

Once, when I was about twelve or thirteen, my mum scolded me for not talking more in class. It was after a parents evening, and two of my teachers said I needed to contribute more to the lessons. My mum asked me why I didn't, but she never actually gave me a chance to reply. I think that was the first time I realised she didn't care much for me anymore; she cared more about the grades. It was then I started to realise she never asked me how I was anymore – she'd just ask about my day. But soon even that turned into a rare comment.

You'd think that my mums constant nagging on doing well would make me try harder. And I did. I poured so much into school. Except it was never enough for her. As far as she was concerned, I wasn't doing anything. I couldn't keep track of the number of times I almost gave up. When all the pressure she was putting on me multiplied when I put more on myself. When I started drowning. When I couldn't cope.

And I think that's a part of the reason I didn't start this earlier. I didn't believe I was strong enough. It didn't matter I'd pushed through endless bullying and other struggles. I still didn't think I had any strength to do anything as monumental as this. It didn't matter that I wanted it so desperately and I'd been daydreaming about a better version of myself. Despite it all, I knew I couldn't do it.

And then, like a switch I didn't know existed being flicked on, I thought, maybe, I could do it. It only needed a second. That was enough for me to think it possible. And once you've started, once you've taken that first great and petrifying leap into the deep end, the rest is easier once you learn how to swim. But you need that split second of belief, of hope, to go forward.

•••

When I walked into tutor the day after, Emily was already sat down, doodling on a scrap piece of paper. Before I even quite knew what I was doing, I walked over, but instead of walking past her desk and onto mine, I stopped in front of her. "Hey, Emily. Could I sit here?"

She looked surprised for a moment, but then smiled widely, the gratitude shown clearly on her face. She said yes, and I dropped my bag on the floor and slid into the chair next to her.

I started to ask how she was, but before I even said anything, I could see she was upset. Really upset. I didn't know if I should ask about it, or grace her with ignorance, pretending I didn't notice. But that felt so wrong.

"Hey, are you ok?" I hoped to sound gentle and kind, and, with some luck, I got close to that.

Emily blinked a few times as if trying to comprehend what I asked, or trying to come up with an answer. After a moment, she simply shook her head, looking me in the eye with so much sadness it almost ate away at me. There was hardly anyone in the room, and they were too absorbed in their games on their phones to notice me pull Emily into a hug while she cried silently against my shoulder.

"It'll be ok, I promise," I whispered. I didn't know that, for sure, but I felt she needed to hear it, and it most likely would be ok eventually. She pulled back after a while and wiped her eyes with the back of her hand before I handed her a tissue from my bag.

I waited another few moments, then ventured to ask if she wanted to talk about it. She considered this, then said, "I've lost my friends."

"What do you mean?" I asked gently.

"They said they didn't want to be friends with me anymore. That I wasn't… that I didn't fit into their group anymore." Tears brimmed in her eyes again, adding a shimmering glint to her hazel eyes, and it was clear she was struggling to keep them from spilling over onto her cheeks like a stream.

"Why, what happened?" I asked, in an attempt to both understand what happened myself and also help her to express her feelings which were so clearly starting to take over.

She looked suddenly scared to say anything, panic written all over her face, so I scrambled and said, "You don't have to say anything if you don't want to."

She gave an apologetic smile, but said, in a small voice, "I just… I told them something and they didn't like it very much."

I struggled to think of what could have been so awful that all her friends would abandon her, but I could see she wasn't going to tell me any more than she already had. I didn't blame her; I knew what it was like to be so scared of losing someone you had to tread on eggshells in fear of saying something you'd regret.

I had no idea what to say, or how to even start to comfort her. But I gave her another hug, and then when we pulled away, I looked at her and said, "It'll be alright."

She smiled at me, weakly, but a smile all the same, and I smiled back, asking if she'd meet at the picnic benches at break and lunch so we could spend the time together. She couldn't have even thought about it in the time it took her to respond, saying she was looking forward to it.

We fell into a pattern after that day. I never sat in my old seat in tutor anymore: I sat next to Emily instead, getting considerably less work done, but I didn't mind. I did it at home instead. We met up every day at break and lunch and we walked between classes together whenever it worked with our timetable – which was quite often. I found myself enjoying it more and more, relaxing and being myself with her in a way I hadn't done for a long time. I hadn't even felt like it when I was friends with Jane and the comfort of having a close friend like that surprised me. We became closer, sharing things about ourselves and learning each other's quirks and mannerisms.

George even joined us at lunch sometimes – the frequency seemed to be increasing with time, too. He'd stride up to our table – always the same one: the one I used to sit at alone, the one George and I sat at that first lunchtime and now mine and Emily's table – and plonk his bag down and sit next to me, with Emily opposite me as always. We'd established a close friendship among the three of us, in the few weeks since I'd become closer to Emily, and I was immensely grateful for it.

I felt so glad that I'd started to come out of myself. Because, although I'd been vulnerable to them both and put myself in a position where they could hurt me, I didn't mind. Because now that I'd gotten real friends, I realised – almost embarrassingly – that I'd been so daft to think that having no one was a better option than risking sadness. Because you risked joy, too. This burning, lightweight and thrilling feeling that I didn't even realise I was missing.

6

With the help of Emily and George, I'd started to contribute more in lessons and talk to other people more, putting myself out there in ways I never had before. In ways I didn't think I could. But, somehow having Emily, and becoming closer to George as the days went on, I now believed that I was capable of becoming the version of myself that I'd always wished I'd be. And, with that new-found knowledge, I had an even greater driving force to push myself out of my comfort zone, out of myself and into the open.

Because this was a thousand times better than the shell I used to be. This felt like freedom and weightlessness while it used to feel like a prison and lead on my shoulders. After I'd gotten over the initial terror of starting something new, something different, and putting myself out there in a way I never had before, the reward was far greater than the discomfort elicited from trying it. And, oddly, it seemed I felt more at ease now, putting myself out there, than I did when I was hiding. I was less scared, despite the fact I was doing things which were scarier.

After Emily and I had spent almost every day together for a few weeks, and the weather was starting to become colder as October took hold, she asked what had changed.

"What do you mean?" I asked, knowing what she was talking about but wanting to buy some time to think of an answer.

"You don't hide within yourself anymore. It was barely a few weeks ago when I hardly got a smile from you in tutor, and now you're smiling to everyone like it's no big deal and you've been doing it for ages, when we both know something's changed." She smiled at me from across the table at lunch, while I picked at my food, uninterested. There was a slight breeze in the air, and a gust whipped my hair around my face as I attempted to tame it back.

I didn't say anything for a minute, and Emily sat there patiently, waiting for me to answer.

Finally, I said, "I couldn't go on like that: never doing anything and hiding behind everyone else so as not to ever be seen. Something changed inside me and I knew I owed it to myself to become something more. I thought that there had to be more than what there was."

Emily didn't say anything for a moment, then she smiled at me and reached across the table to squeeze my hand, and then seemingly decided that wasn't enough. She pulled me up and I stepped over the bench and walked around the table so I was next to her and she pulled me into a hug, wrapping her arms around me. I felt so safe there, and at that moment I knew I'd done the right thing, despite feeling as though I couldn't continue on way too many occasions. Because although the benefits were amazing, the worry and fear were still prominent and it sometimes became hard to ignore.

She pulled back and smiled at me again, and before she let me go completely, she said, "Well, I'm glad you decided to come out of yourself. I like this you."

•••

Emily and I were coming out of art together, laughing at our poor attempts to draw a human figure in the lesson — which, we both decided, we weren't going to use in our final project because apparently, you could draw faces with ease, but the body was much harder — when some of Emily's old friends walked past. We saw them at the same time, and we both stopped laughing abruptly, Emily stumbling a little at the sight of those she used to be so close to. I looked from the girls to Emily and noticed that Emily looked away, refusing to meet their eyes. We stood, almost as a standoff, and I realised I'd moved to stand between them, to shield Emily from whatever harm they may throw at her.

I took Emily's hand in my own, and feeling a new sort of protectiveness over her, pulled her away from them to walk in the opposite direction. I felt a small resistance on her part, but she soon followed me. We weren't headed that way, but I didn't care if we had to walk further. All I cared about in that moment was getting Emily away from their piercing and judging stares. Because I knew exactly how that felt. Before we turned the corner, I heard the girls sniggering at our backs, but it only fuelled my anger at them and my friendship towards Emily, and I sped up determinedly.

The idea of Emily feeling like I did for months made my skin crawl.

"Hey, it'll be ok." I stopped walking and pulled Emily to the wall so we were out of the way of the main stream of students. Her eyes shone a little with the effort of holding back tears and she refused to look me in the eye, either from embarrassment or something else, I couldn't tell. Her eyes flicked around, barely resting on one spot for more than a second.

A few people sneaked curious glances at us, so I led her back into the stream of students so we could make our way somewhere quieter. It was lunch, so we turned at the door to go outside and made our way to the picnic tables. We didn't talk until we got there, Emily gratefully slouching into the bench, not even bothering to take her bag off at first. I sat opposite her and squeezed her arm from across the table, hopefully letting her know I was there for her.

"Screw them. They never deserved you anyway," I said, trying to keep the anger from rising within me. I needed to be there for Emily, and I couldn't do that if I let my emotions take over. I pushed down the memories of Jane and her new friends looking at me like Emily's old friends did, unwilling to revisit those moments now.

She looked up, finally meeting my eye, and smiled a little, the corners of her mouth hardly lifting, but it was a start. I wasn't sure of the best way to make her feel better, and I struggled for a moment on what to say.

But before I could say anything, Emily started talking quietly, in a rush, like she had to get the words out before a certain time. "I was happy with them, you know. I thought they cared for me and that they wanted me around. I thought I could tell them anything and it wouldn't change our friendship. We were close. I just wanted to tell them," she faltered, her breath catching like she was stopping herself from saying too much at the last moment. "I wanted them to know me better. And it blew up in my face."

Tears had started to fall down her cheeks, and she hastily wiped them away with her fingers. "Why was I so stupid?" She asked, almost wistfully.

"Hey. Hey." I waited for her to look at me, then continued. "This was not your fault. Okay? You are not the one to blame for this. I don't know what you told them and I'm not going to ask," — I'd learnt she'd tell me when she was ready, pushing her wouldn't lead to anything — "but whatever it was, it's their fault for caring too much about one detail. You're amazing. You're lovely and kind and caring and you make me laugh and I don't care what it was, I promise it won't change anything between us if you do ever want to tell me."

This time, she really smiled. Even through her tears, she was smiling widely and the relief was clear in her face.

"Thank you. Thank you so, so much."

And that was all I needed. I got up and hugged her, holding her to me as if she could float away. She wiped away the last of her tears as we pulled back, but her eyes were still red and puffy.

"Plus," I said, smiling, "if they ever even look at you the wrong way, I'll be ready to punch their faces in." I was only half-joking. I wasn't a violent person, but I realised, in that moment, that I didn't want Emily to get hurt and I would do a lot to make sure that didn't happen.

She laughed, and the sound made it impossible for me not to laugh too.

I knew Emily wasn't exactly happy in that moment, but I could tell she wasn't as upset as she had been. Her face wasn't as clouded by the past, and her eyes had lost the shimmering gleam of fresh tears.

We had just sat back down when I spotted George out of the corner of my eye, walking towards us. I estimated we had about thirty seconds until he reached us.

"Do you want to come back to mine tonight? After school, I mean," I blurted. I wanted to ask before George came, to try to reduce the awkwardness.

I was immediately glad I asked. Emily's face lit up so brightly it could have been a torch on the dark. "Yes, definitely. Let me just ask my parents." She pulled out her phone and typed out a text quickly, then put it on the table, awaiting a response. I'd already asked my mum if I could bring a friend home, and I think she was so surprised I'd asked — or that I even had a friend — that she said yes.

I hadn't had a friend round in so long, and though I could remember the last time with a horrible sense of sadness and betrayal, I was so excited at the concept I could barely hide my delight at her enthusiasm too.

Emily's phone screen lit up barely a few seconds later, just as George came and flopped down in the seat next to me. As he sat down, he casually laid his hand on my shoulder for a moment, saying hello to us both. I tried to hide my shock, stuttering out a hello. But I couldn't hide the blush which spread across my cheeks at his touch, which I prayed he didn't notice. He was at least polite enough not to mention it.

Emily noticed though. She raised a sly eyebrow at me, but looked down at her phone and smiled. "Yes, my mum said yes. What's your address?"

I held my hand out for the phone, and I typed in my address as George asked what was going on.

"Emily's coming round to mine tonight," I said simply.

George nodded, almost approvingly. Then he looked at Emily, really looked it seemed. "Hey, are you ok?" He asked, sounding genuinely concerned. Her eyes were still a little red.

Emily looked at George, then at me for a moment and smiled. "Yeah, I'm ok now."

And the gratitude and friendship held in her voice made my heart swell. Because I'd created that: I'd helped her feel better and I felt oddly proud of myself for doing so.

George looked as if he was about to say more, then changed his mind. Then changed his mind again, opening his mouth to say, "Well, I'm glad."

Emily and I smiled at each other, then she looked down at her phone again, getting back to the matter of coming round mine. "Hey! You live, like, a five-minute walk from me," she said enthusiastically. My jaw almost dropped.

"What?"

"Yeah, I live here," she said, pointing to the map she'd brought up on her phone, "and you're there." She pointed again. And she was right: it was just around the corner from me. I couldn't believe we hadn't realised that before, we could have spent more time together already. And to think this amazing friend I'd found had always been so close to me made me dizzy.

I didn't know how to express what I was feeling, but I smiled broadly, hoping it conveyed everything.

George just looked between us both, seemingly confused at what was happening between us until we veered to a different conversation he could be included in.

As lunch went on, I saw more and more sadness leave Emily and she became more relaxed, laughing more easily with George and I. I got the feeling we were both stealing glances at each other: me to make sure she was alright, and her to try and figure out what had happened between George and me earlier.

But I made sure I still tried to keep her spirits up, which, in a way, boosted mine too. I couldn't let any of my own sadness or worries or insecurities show, and the forced happiness almost fooled even me that it was true.

Not that, anymore, I really had anything to be particularly upset or worried about. I had Emily and George, and I was getting closer to each of them — almost to the point where I started to wonder if something really could happen between George and I — and I felt safe with them: confident in the fact that they wanted me around and liked my company. I was no longer entirely lonely, I had someone to look out for and who looked out for me. Nobody had said anything bad to me for a while now, but the memory of what had happened previously and the threat of what could still happen hung around me like a cloud.

But then, why was I still worried about what people thought of me? Why was I not happier? Why did I still feel so damn scared of losing my friends?

7

Waiting by the school gates for Emily, I desperately tried to reassure myself that everything would be alright. But the memory of what had happened the last time I had a friend round my house was imprinted in my mind and I couldn't shake the feeling that this time wouldn't go well either.

But I tried to remind myself that Emily was not Jane, and Emily wouldn't hurt me. Even in the few weeks we'd been close friends, I knew that fact more strongly than I ever had in the three years I'd been friends with Jane. Somehow, with Emily, I didn't doubt our friendship so much. It was only in my darker moments that I questioned whether Emily even liked me or wanted me as a friend. Normally, though, I felt that it was a given that I'd be friends with Emily and that she'd be there for me. But with Jane, I never felt particularly comfortable or secure in our friendship, like it was something that was always about to end: it was only a matter of time.

And, most importantly, I knew that Emily wasn't about to dump me — from a friendship, that is — like

Jane did the last time I'd had a friend round, almost eight months ago.

By the time Emily walked up to me, apologising somewhat profusely for keeping me waiting, I had composed myself. And the sight of her smiling face calmed and silenced any worries I may have had, and I couldn't help but grin at her.

She looked much happier than she had at lunch, her smile easier and her eyes no longer held the cloud of misery. I wondered, briefly, if inviting her to my house had helped to dispel that fog. The thought made my heart swell.

There were a few seats left on the bus when we got on, and we took two near the back, farther back than I normally would have sat. We chatted for the whole journey, non-consequential things like music and books, and we shared my earphones to listen to music on my phone. And there was something in that, listening to the same song through the same earphones that was oddly intimate: like I somehow knew another part of Emily and we'd become closer. I looked up at her to see her reaction to the songs I was playing her, and seeing her lips pull into a smile made me feel like I'd achieved something. Something small, but something nonetheless.

I thought maybe this was what having a real friend was like.

And I thought how much I'd missed from closing myself off, and I was briefly angry at myself for being so ignorant and stubborn. But I stopped myself, looking at Emily and hearing her voice to try to not dwell on the past. I couldn't change how I'd acted, but I could change how I'd act in the future.

And I thought I would make sure I didn't stop myself from feeling happiness again; I'd let myself feel.

●●●

I unhooked the latch on the gate and held it open for Emily to walk through. "My lady," I said, dipping my head like a servant in Downtown Abbey. She laughed abruptly, like she had no hope or will of containing it. We'd hardly gotten a few steps up the path when Pumpkin came bounding up to us, barking loudly.

"It's only me, Pumpkin." She pushed her nose against my hand and I stroked her head, rubbing behind her ears as she leant against me.

"Emily, meet Pumpkin. Pumpkin, Emily."

I came up with her name. We got her when she was just a puppy, from an animal rescue centre, around Halloween and we had a pumpkin sitting by the fireplace. We still hadn't thought of a name for her, so I just said: "How about Pumpkin?" In an almost sarcastic tone of voice, half knowing that my parents wouldn't like it, but hoping they would. But before they could even give their opinion, she came bounding up to us and started sniffing the pumpkin vigorously, and we all laughed at how perfect the name was for her.

"Hey, Pumpkin." Pumpkin whipped her head around, noticing Emily for the first time, and proceeded to sniff her determinedly. Emily laughed, and I started to walk up the path, with Emily and Pumpkin close behind. I unlocked the door and let Emily walk in first.

My mum was just coming around the corner as I closed the door behind me.

"Hi, mum. This is Emily," I said simply, hoping she wouldn't launch into a thousand questions.

"Hi," Emily said, waving somewhat awkwardly. I was half glad to see that I wasn't the only one who became awkward around friends' parents, but I also knew how uncomfortable it was, so I pleaded silently to my mum not to over complicate things.

"Nice to meet you, Emily. I'm Molly." My mum smiled, and it didn't look like she was going to converse much more with us, thank God.

"You too."

"We're going upstairs," I said to my mum, and she just nodded before smiling at Emily.

"Make yourself at home," she said warmly, more warmly than was usual for her.

"Thank you."

And with that, I pointed out where Emily could leave her shoes, then led her upstairs to my room, pointing out the bathroom as we went.

"Sit anywhere," I said, gesturing vaguely to my chair, bed and the floor. She nodded, looked around, then sat on the floor, crossing her legs beneath her. I sat down opposite her as she looked around.

"I love your room. Did you draw those?" She was looking at the pin-board I had on my wall, full of sketches and drawings I'd done. There was a note of admiration in her voice.

"Um, yeah," I said, slightly embarrassed.

"They're really good. Like, really, really good." She smiled at me sweetly.

I couldn't help but grin back, and said, "Thank you."

I'd been complimented on my drawings before, but never so outwardly or with so much admiration and never by someone, other than my parents, who meant so much to me.

We sat in companionable silence for a moment, then Emily said, with a mischievous glint in her eyes, "So, George."

"What about him?" I said, feigning confusion.

She gave me a lopsided smile. "You like him, don't you?"

I opened my mouth. Then closed it again. "Someone's observant," I said, instead of outright answering her question.

She gave a little squeal, and I lightly flicked her arm. "Awhhh this is so cute, I can't even."

I let her have a little fangirl moment, then said, "It's nothing. He doesn't like me so nothing's going to happen." Admitting it hurt more than I would have liked.

She stared at me for a second, her mouth open. "Are you blind?" When I looked at her, dumbfounded, she carried on. "Have you even seen the way he looks at you? You're not the only one who wants something to happen."

I didn't know what to say, but I was smiling despite myself. I didn't want to get my hopes up, because what if Emily misread the signs? And even if he did like me, that doesn't mean he'd want anything to happen.

"You should tell him." I looked up at her, shocked. Because I couldn't think of anything worse. At least, I couldn't at first. And then I thought about it. And maybe it wouldn't be the worst thing. Because if he really did like me, and wanted to get together, isn't that exactly what I wanted? I'd fantasised about us being together, and now it really might be a possibility, I couldn't believe it.

"What if it ruins our friendship?" I said at last.

"What if it doesn't?"

That stumped me.

I remembered what I'd thought earlier on the bus, how I'd let myself feel. And now I had an opportunity to do that, and I was backing away.

"Ok," I said before I could change my mind. Don't overthink it, I told myself.

"You could text him?" Emily suggested. Maybe she saw the worry written on my face.

Texting would be easier. That's for sure. But a part of me felt like it was cheating, taking the easy option. I said as much to Emily, and she thought about it for a moment.

"That's ok. It doesn't have to be hard. People do stuff like this over text all the time." I didn't know if she was right, but it did make the idea seem better. I felt I could do it, if it was texting. After all, I'd only just recently started talking more and coming out of myself, it seemed fair that I had an easier option to take.

It wasn't long before I was almost excited at the thought. Terrified, but excited too. Because maybe it was going to be my chance to really know what I was capable of and to achieve one of the things I'd been too scared to in the past.

Once I'd gotten over the initial panic of it, it was starting to look like a good idea.

"So, what about you? Do you like anyone?" I asked Emily. I almost laughed at the cliché of this whole conversation, but I didn't care.

She blushed, unable to hide the fact that there clearly was someone. Now it was my time to squeal.

"Who is it?"

But Emily suddenly stopped smiling and she looked on the verge of tears. "Hey, what's wrong?" I said, placing my hand on her arm.

She didn't reply, just looked at me, as if trying to decide whether to say anything or not. I let her think, not speaking but staying where I was so she knew I was there for her.

She wiped away the few stray tears which had fallen, and it looked like she'd finished some internal battle. Whether she lost or won, I couldn't tell.

She took a deep breath, then looked at me, but didn't meet my eyes.

"It's a girl."

She peeked up to see my reaction. I smiled at her broadly. "What's her name?" I asked.

She let out a breath which I assume she'd been holding. The relief on her face was so obvious it almost broke my heart. She was clearly so worried about how I'd react, whether I'd be ok with it or not, that she was seemingly beyond relief that I was alright with it. My heart gave a painful lurch at the idea of her having to feel this fear every time she had to tell a new person, and of the shit she'd have to face when it went wrong. I wanted to shield her from it all, but I knew I couldn't.

"Anna. She's in our art," Emily said, a smile lighting up her face.

I let out a small squeal again, feeling about twelve, but not caring. "I sit near her in German; she's really nice."

I couldn't stop smiling. I was just so happy for Emily and so proud of her that she'd come out to me.

But then I stopped short. "Wait. Is this what you told your old friends?" I almost didn't want to know the answer.

She nodded slightly. "Yeah. We were at Taylor's house and talking about crushes, and I told them I'm gay. And they flipped out. Saying they wanted nothing to do with me and it was wrong and disgusting. They kicked me out, and I had to walk a couple of miles home." Emily seemed so deflated.

I hugged her, knowing I couldn't say anything to make it better.

"I was so, so scared to tell you. I didn't want the same thing happening. But I decided I'd rather know now and be myself with you, rather than hide it and find out later that it's a deal-breaker for you."

I shook my head, pulling back so I could look her in the eye. "I don't care if you're gay or not. I don't care who you love. As long as you're happy; that's all I care about. You should always be yourself. Don't hide who you are just because some people don't like it. Screw them. It's your life."

I meant every word.

It made me angry, though, that her old friends would let her go simply because of one tiny part of her. It's like hating someone for liking art or football. Emily just liked girls instead of boys, and there's nothing wrong with that. Now I really wanted to punch them. Of course, people can have their own opinions, but it shouldn't get in the way of a friendship.

I hated the world for being so stubborn and conservative about everything, hating anything unlike themselves, and for making such a huge deal of something so inconsequential.

"Have you told anyone else?" I asked.

She shook her head. "Just my old friends and you. I haven't told my parents yet."

I nodded. "Do you want to?"

"I don't know. I mean, I don't really want to hide who I am anymore. But I'm scared. Like, I'm not sure how my parents will take it and I'm scared to face any of the crap I'll get at school." She stopped for a minute, looking like she was trying to compose herself. "And I'm scared that my old friends will out me."

"Do they have a reason to?" I asked gently.

"They have no reason not to."

"I know this is clichéd, but you can't know what will happen until it happens. There's no point in being worried about something that you have no way of controlling. Everyone will react how they react; when it happens won't change their response." Maybe I should have taken some of my own advice.

I knew I had no right to try to help. After all, I was straight and this was something I wouldn't experience for myself. But I wanted to help. I hated seeing her so upset and all I wanted was for her to be happy and be herself.

Emily just nodded, in thought.

"Just, know that I'm here for you, ok? I know I'm straight, so all of what I'm saying probably doesn't count. I won't ever experience the same things you are, or will, but I want to at least try to help. And if all I can do is just be here, then that's ok."

"Thank you for understanding," she said gratefully.

"Of course. So, do you want to talk about all this? I'm guessing you haven't been able to talk about it all that much?"

"Yeah, that'd be really nice actually. But first. I'm glad you're ok with it. I would have been sad to see you go. I'm happier with you and George than I ever was before. I'm really glad you talked to me that day, so thanks." She looked almost sheepish, showing this rare affection.

"You know, I was just thinking earlier how much happier I am with you guys than I was before too. So maybe we all helped each other."

"Maybe." She hugged me again, for my benefit or hers, I wasn't sure.

"Also, George would be cool with it. You know Bradley Lucas? He's in George's band? He's gay, and out, and George is totally fine with it. So were most people, I think. He's really nice, maybe you could talk to him if you wanted someone who knew what it was like?" I suggested. I thought that the knowledge that her other close friend wouldn't mind would be comforting, at least a little.

Emily nodded and smiled, and said, "Yeah, maybe. Thanks."

But she did talk to me about it all too, how she had a pretty good idea she was gay when she was thirteen and then questioned and doubted herself for a year before coming to grips with it. How she still felt, sometimes, that she should change and that it was wrong (to which I said, "Never change who you are. You're not wrong, you're just you."). How it was all so confusing when she couldn't talk to anyone about it because she didn't trust anyone enough. And how, now, she was just left being scared of what might happen.

And through all of it, she didn't once look ashamed or embarrassed of who she was. I thought I should try and take something from that: just be yourself, always.

8

Today was the day. The day where I told George that he made butterflies dance in my stomach and made me lose my train of thought. That he made the world stop spinning.

My insides started doing flips the moment he texted me — first. Which meant he was thinking about me. Which meant he liked me in some sort of way, right? But I was probably getting ahead of myself, hoping for things I'd promised myself I wouldn't hope for, no matter what Emily said. It was the first day of the October half term, the Friday we broke up from school for a week, and I'd planned to tell George how I felt over the weekend. So when he asked me if I liked anyone, I was momentarily confused. I didn't expect for him to broach the subject — I thought I'd have to awkwardly, and as casually as possible, fit it in. But there was no need. I thought I might as well tell him now, it was the perfect opportunity.

So, after swallowing down the terror and the rising panic, I said that yes, there was someone who took up a large portion of my thoughts. I was tactfully vague, to start with. At least until he asked who? And then all of the vague tactfulness was thrown out of the window to be forgotten.

I typed out the letters slowly, carefully, deliberately and stared at the short word for a few moments. My thumb hovered over the send button for a short time. Then, before I could change my mind or talk myself out of it, I pressed the button.

I watched the bar creep along the top of the screen, holding my breath. Then I watched the small bubble, containing "you" inside of it. Three tiny letters that could change everything.

I asked who he liked before he could say anything else. I knew he'd read it, and I was waiting, with my eyes glued on the screen, for the three dots to appear, indicating his typing.

Then when it finally came, and I read his reply, I was almost certain he must have been joking. I reread it over and over. But the three letters didn't change. I waited for the moment he sent a laughing emoji or said he was joking. But it never came. My heart sped up to what must have been dangerous, and I felt my lips pull into a smile, reaching my eyes.

I finally let myself believe him. It's what I wanted, after all. It's what I was secretly longing for, even though I thought it was impossible. Even though Emily was so convinced he liked me too, I refused to let myself believe it. But there it was. You. We both said the same thing.

You.

Why would a boy like George like a girl like me?

But, we talked for hours on end. I couldn't even believe that he wanted to talk to me for that long. We'd never talked for more than an hour at a time. And, I swear, I didn't get used to seeing his name on my screen for so long. And the flipping and turning of my stomach never stopped or even dulled — in fact, it may have intensified. But now, it wasn't out of fear or discomfort. It somehow reminded me of how much this all meant to me and it made me feel alive like I was doing something meaningful and worthwhile.

I discovered that he had actually liked me for quite a while too. I couldn't believe it. All that time I'd been dreaming of him, he'd been dreaming of me too. It was almost too good to be true. But while my thoughts were in a castle in the air, the scepticism shrunk to almost nothing. But there was still a tiny part of me, irrational or not, I didn't know, which knew this wouldn't last. Which thought it was some trick or he didn't really mean it — because why else would he be bothering? As much as I wanted to, I couldn't fully believe he meant all the beautiful things he was saying to me.

But, with some effort, I forced down the pessimistic thoughts and focused only on the joy I was feeling. And I reminded myself how far I'd come. I was talking to the boy who made me feel things so deeply it scared me and I didn't care about what I said, it just felt so comfortable and easy, like I wholeheartedly believed he wouldn't ever think less of me. And that feeling was so new and amazing I felt almost drunk on it.

•••

For the next week of half term, we talked every day. I rang him after the second day when I craved for something more than texts, and the sound of his voice against my ear sent shivers down my spine in a way I never thought possible.

Each conversation was like learning about a new part of George, What he liked, what he didn't, stories of his past. I learnt about his family and his dreams for the future. He told me about what scared him and what he felt passionate about. And I did the same, sharing parts of myself I hadn't to anyone else. And it didn't scare me. I wasn't worried about what he'd think or how he'd react, and I didn't have to filter how I felt for him. I could just be myself.

I wasn't hesitant to tell George how I felt about him. How he made me smile when even breathing felt impossible. How he somehow filled each day with a joy that overruled anything else I might have felt. How he filled me with a hope that had me believing I could be happy; that I deserved happiness. I wasn't hesitant to tell him anything; talking to George was as easy as breathing.

I even told him about my parents, how I felt I couldn't talk to them because I was scared and I thought they didn't care. How they put too much pressure on me to do well in school and how they constantly compared me to my older sister, Grace. And about all that had happened with Jane and how I thought that shutting myself off from everyone and being lonely was a better option than making friends. How scared I was to simply walk down the corridors in school sometimes because the fear of what could happen weighed down my shoulders. How even when I was friends with Jane, it always felt like it wasn't anything real and I could never fully relax with her because I wasn't comfortable or happy. How I was bullied relentlessly at the end of primary school and the beginning of secondary school and I hadn't gotten over it, unable to stop the fear of it happening again and believing what I was told. How much I worried about what other people thought, how other people saw me. I told George how bad everything had gotten in the last few years and how scared I was that it would happen again. How anxiety got the better of me more often than I would've liked to admit. And he comforted me, letting me talk things through in a way that was surprisingly beneficial. It seemed I needed someone like George more than I'd realised.

I'd filled up almost a whole sketchbook with drawings and paintings of faces, all with a different emotion raw on their features. Some I'd drawn with a split down the middle, showing how emotions fought for control and how people often hid how they really felt. I'd sent George photos of some of my favourites and I explained it all to him over FaceTime one night, my thoughts turning into a rambling speech which I felt momentarily embarrassed about before he smiled encouragingly and told me he thought it was cute, how passionate I was about it. My heart melted, and I'd drawn until three the next morning, page after page, unable to stop.

On the Thursday of half term, almost a week after we'd opened up about our feelings, we met at the park. It was about halfway between our two houses, and I walked the twenty minutes it took to get there. I'd told my parents I was meeting a friend, and they hadn't questioned more about it and I didn't volunteer more information. And, technically, it wasn't a lie. We were meeting Emily there a few hours after George and I arranged to meet.

I got there a few minutes early, and I scanned the surroundings for signs of George, but he wasn't there yet. The park had a children's play area where I used to spend a lot of time as a kid, my mum took my sister and me, and then as Grace got older, she'd take me instead. My mum started giving up on things like that, handing the responsibility to my older sister. I didn't realise it until a few years after it all happened, though.

I looked at the swings, now looking like they needed repainting, and smiled to myself at the memory of Grace pushing me into the sky and the feeling of weightlessness which accompanied it. I realised how much I missed her since she moved out when I started secondary school and she left for university.

I turned back around and saw George coming through the gates where we were supposed to be meeting, but I waved at him and he jogged over to me instead. The sight of him hurrying over to me brought a grin to my face, dispelling the nostalgia building up, and I couldn't help but marvel at all the events which led up to this moment: how they all intertwined together to bring someone as amazing as George bounding towards me with a grin on his face, mirroring my own.

And my heart melted.

As he neared me, he held his arms open and I stepped into them when he got to me, letting his arms envelop me. We stood like that for a minute, his body warm against mine, and I felt safe. I felt happy and I thanked a god I didn't believe in for letting the moment happen.

George stepped back and smiled as he looked at me. "Hey, beautiful."

I smiled, a blush blossoming on my cheeks, and I was acutely aware of his hand holding mine like it was the most natural thing. And it felt natural, my hand fit into his and I liked the feeling of his skin against mine. "Hey, handsome."

"Shall we walk?"

I nodded and, with our fingers still entwined together, we walked down the path to the clearing, beyond the children's play area. There were benches at regular intervals, and we sat down on one next to a tree that was in the sun, which held little heat but felt comforting on my skin.

We talked easily, and, thankfully, there wasn't any of the awkwardness I feared there might be. I wasn't used to feeling so comfortable talking with someone, but I wasn't complaining. It was a nice feeling, freeing, like I hadn't realised I'd been waiting for exactly this. I wondered if George felt similar.

I didn't know if it was ok to question his past relationships, but I did anyway. "Have you been with anyone before?"

He looked at me sideways, like he was trying to gauge why I'd asked. "Unless you count a three-day relationship in year two, then no, I haven't." He laughed a little as if embarrassed by his seven-year-old self. "Have you?"

I had to hold back a laugh because the idea I'd ever had a boyfriend sounded so ridiculous. "No, not even a three-day relationship in year two."

"We're in the same boat, then," George said, gently shoving my arm playfully.

I laughed, then nodded. "I guess so."

I felt oddly comforted by this fact, that I wasn't groping my way in the dark alone.

•••

We got lunch at the café in the middle of the park, and we shared a strawberry milkshake afterwards, with two straws, something surprisingly intimate but somehow thrilling. We walked around the park, weaving through trees and bushes, holding hands.

Stopping under a tree, we sat down on the grass around the roots. I leant my head on his shoulder as he wrapped his arm around me, and we didn't say anything for a minute. The birds around us sung cheerfully, communicating with each other in extraordinary ways. We moved so we were leaning against the trunk of a tree, so ginormous we were still side by side.

I looked up into his eyes, and he looked into mine. I thought about kissing him. I could do it easily: all it would take was a stretch of my neck and our lips would meet. But I didn't know if I was ready and I didn't want to ruin what we had. I wanted to take it slow, or at least not rush into anything.

So, instead, I looked away and shuffled down, resting my head on his chest as he played with my hair, running his fingers through the strands. We had another twenty minutes before Emily came and, for now, I was content to just be there with George, faintly feeling his heartbeat through his shirt and knowing this was something good.

9

Looking around me, I tried not to worry about the fact that George was now ten minutes late to lunch and he hadn't replied to my messages since last night. I tried to tell myself there were plenty of logical reasons. Maybe he had to talk to a teacher or do something for his music project. Maybe he'd left his phone at home or he didn't have any signal. But no number of potential reasons quietened my racing thoughts. I had to focus on Emily to keep the panic from taking over, but even then, my fingers were anxiously tapping the table and I'd hardly touched my food.

Emily, observant as always, noticed my agitation, but she didn't press it when I said it was nothing.

After another couple of minutes, just as I was starting to give up hope that George would show up, I saw him step outside. I smiled involuntarily, but as he neared us, my smile faded.

He didn't look happy. In fact, he looked conflicted, anger and sadness fighting over his features. I saw him work to compose his features into an arrangement which conveyed nothing, hiding his true feelings.

I'd plastered a smile onto my face by the time George came over. I pretended I hadn't seen what had been going on in his head just a few seconds previously.

"Hey," I said, as he sat down next to me. He didn't touch me. Not even a hand on my shoulder. I tried not to bristle.

"Hi," George said, in forced cheeriness. He nodded hello to Emily before turning back to me slightly. "You alright?"

"I'm good, you?"

"Fine."

I didn't know what to say. I hadn't known George to be so blunt. I used to be the blunt one, giving little information, before I stepped out of myself. I wasn't used to being on the receiving end.

I glanced at Emily to find her looking between us, the questions clearly written on her face. I wished I knew the answers.

I asked him about his day, but he never elaborated, even after I prompted him. I told him about mine, though he hadn't asked.

"Are you sure you're ok?" I asked gently, after I couldn't take it anymore. I put my hand on his arm, and he looked at it as if assessing whether or not to push me off. He didn't, though.

He didn't say anything, and I thought he was going to tell me. But then his face clouded over even more, and he said, "I'm fine."

I knew he wasn't, but I didn't want to push him either.

He looked up at me, then like something inside him changed, he grabbed his bag from the floor and stood up. "I've got to go."

He was already up and a few steps away by the time it registered, and I rushed up and over to him, saying his name. He didn't turn around. I grabbed hold of his wrist and he spun around, looking so angry that I almost flinched back.

"What's going on? You can talk to me, you know." It almost sounded like I was pleading.

"I'm sorry," he said, then he pulled out of my grasp with a force that left me stunned and turned around, walking so quickly it surprised me. This time, I let him go, watching him hurry away.

I was worried about him, but I was so shocked too. We'd been talking the day before, at school, the first day back after half term, and everything had been like normal. And now, all of a sudden, it's like I was too much for him. And that look. Like he couldn't bear to see me. It almost broke me.

I walked back to the table, and slumped down next to Emily, leaning against her shoulder.

"What happened?" Emily asked kindly, concern laced into her voice.

I shook my head. "I have no idea."

•••

I didn't see George again that day. But I couldn't stop thinking about what happened at lunch. We'd only been sort-of-together for little over a week, and already he hated the sight of me. And the worst thing was, I didn't know what had happened. And I was scared to ask.

At the end of the day, as I was getting off the bus with Emily — she got the bus with me now, since her mum had changed jobs and couldn't drive Emily in anymore — I texted George, simply saying hello and asking what had happened earlier.

"Can we go somewhere other than home, please?" I asked Emily. I wanted to be out, not confined to the four walls of my room where I could worry and agonise over George.

"Sure. Where?" Emily replied, immediately understanding.

I shrugged, and Emily suggested the woods. I nodded and followed her as she led the way. We didn't talk until we got there, sitting under the trees, surrounded by branches and leaves, giving us cover from anyone walking nearby.

"So, how are things going with Anna?" I asked. I didn't want to talk about George: I needed a distraction of some sort, and asking about Emily's love life seemed like the perfect thing.

Her eyes immediately lit up at the mention of Anna. I smiled, happy to see her so happy.

"Good, I think. We've been talking a lot, actually. I'm still trying to figure out if she's gay, though," Emily said. She was smiling, seemingly despite herself and without realising.

"Does she know you're gay?" I ventured.

Emily shook her head. "Well, I don't think so anyway. I haven't told her."

"Maybe you should?" At the panicked look on Emily's face, I continued. "Look, you like this girl a lot, don't you?"

Emily nodded. "Like, so much it's scary."

"I think you should tell her that. Or flirt with her, or make a move. Just… something."

Emily didn't say anything, clearly lost in thought. Then she looked up at me, worry in her eyes. "What if she doesn't like me back?"

I smiled, remembering what Emily said to me when we were talking about George. "What if she does?"

A smile flittered across her face, and I hoped she realised how I'd turned her own words to help her.

"You never know, maybe she's just waiting for you to make the first move."

"Maybe." She smiled again, but wider now, like she was seriously considering what could happen between the two of them.

"You got this," I said and wrapped my arms around her. "And, if she breaks your heart, she will have my wrath to deal with. And she won't want that."

Emily laughed, and I joined her and, for a moment, I forgot that I was worried about what might happen between George and I.

10

Sitting on the bus at the end of the day, with my music playing too loudly, I thought about how George didn't say anything when we passed in the hallway that day like I wasn't there. And how he stormed off at lunch on Tuesday like he couldn't bear to look at me. How he hasn't replied to my texts since then, and I hadn't even seen him on Wednesday or Thursday. My stomach twisted uncomfortably, my panic becoming more and more prominent and my thoughts turning to dread.

And that's when all the doubts and worries crashed in: what if he never meant those things? What if he felt differently about me? What if he's thought it over and, somehow, he can't do it, can't do us, anymore? I hoped I was overreacting — but I knew better. I shouldn't have gotten my hopes up as I had, and I was going to pay for that.

I'd felt so secure and safe in what I had with George, that I thought I'd lulled myself into a false sense of security.

But I had to try. I had to know what was going on.

•••

So, the moment I arrived home from school that Friday, exactly two weeks after we'd told each other how we felt, I sent a simple text saying, "Hi," to George with a few kisses afterwards. I left it a minute, then before he'd replied or even seen it, I typed out another message and sent it before I could change my mind. "Is everything ok? Please talk to me."

I tried to read or draw while I waited for George to reply. But I couldn't. I was too scared, too worried, too wound up to do anything except stare at the screen waiting for the three dots: typing.

When he did finally reply, my throat was in my mouth.

George: Call me.

I scrambled to pull up his contact to phone him, my heart pounding.

He answered on the first ring.

"Zoe?" He sounded upset, even in those two syllables.

"Yeah?" I was going to be open-minded to start with, at least. I was going to give him a chance for him to explain.

He launched in, not waiting for more prompts from me. "I'm sorry. I freaked out. Tom said something stupid on Monday's band practise and, to be honest, I got scared. Scared that we were going too fast and I'd ruin it and I'd hurt you and you'd hate me, and I'd never forgive myself. And I couldn't bear that, and I didn't know what to do but I know I probably did the wrong thing and I've done exactly what I promised myself I wouldn't. So I'm sorry. I'm really sorry. Could you forgive me?" The pain was clear in his voice, and I could tell how much this was all upsetting him. And George, who normally spoke so calmly, was stumbling over his words.

I waited a moment before I spoke. "On one condition," I said, already knowing exactly how I felt about all this.

"Of course. What is it?" George was so eager to make it better that I knew I'd made the right choice.

"Just, the next time you're scared or worried, or when we're going too fast or it all gets crazy, don't push me away. Tell me, let me in and let me help. We can work it out together. Just, don't run away again, ok?" I hoped I sounded less scared than I felt.

"Ok, ok. I'll try, I promise. I'll try really hard to not run away," said George, the conviction and determination clear.

"Good. I'll help too, you know. Because, for the record, freaking out is kind of my thing." I was only half-joking.

He laughed, and I felt the tension drain out of me. "So, we're cool?" He asked.

"Yeah, we're cool."

"I want to hug you so badly right now," George said wistfully.

"God, me too." I smiled and felt tears well in my eyes. One slowly escaped, making a small trail down my cheek. I wiped at it and blinked back the rest. I didn't want to cry, I was happy. I didn't care if they were happy tears, I didn't want tears at all.

We started talking again in the same way as we did in the holidays, and all my worries and doubts from earlier evaporated away.

"You know," I started, after we'd been talking for over an hour, and had switched to FaceTime halfway through, "I was terrified. Before I spoke up more and came out of myself a bit, I was so, so terrified. I still am. It's scary, doing something new and different. I worried I'd do something wrong or make a fool of myself or something. But I pushed through that fear and did it all anyway. And nothing went wrong. Things went very right, actually. Because if I hadn't done it, I never would have been friends with Emily, and I probably wouldn't be with you.

"My point is, things are scary. Life is so damn scary, but you do it anyway. And you get some great things from it, I think. So, when things get scary, don't stop."

George was looking at me through the screen with a tilted smile on his face. "That was very inspirational, Zoe."

I blushed. "Yeah, well."

"And, for the record, I think something would have happened between us. I noticed you even when you were trying to be invisible. How could I not?" His voice was so soft and caring, meaning every word.

I beamed at him, unable to do anything else, and my heart swelled.

He carried on before I had a chance to say anything. "I wanted to find out about you, to know all about you," he paused as if trying to convince himself to say something. "I wanted to talk to you so much more than we did, but I could see how uncomfortable you were and I hated to see you like that. All I really wanted was to make you feel comfortable with me, even with yourself. I wanted to help, I just didn't know how."

I shook my head, but I couldn't stop myself from smiling. I knew he'd liked me before we became closer, but I didn't realise how much. Or how much he noticed or cared about me. Warmth flooded through me, and for the tenth time that day, I thanked my lucky stars.

"I didn't expect any help. I knew I had to do it myself, for it to be mine. And you say I was uncomfortable with you, you should have seen me with other people. And with you, I had the butterflies to contend with, too."

He laughed, but I hadn't meant it as a joke. I was being serious, but I didn't say anything about it.

"Seriously though, I did like talking with you. I liked spending time with you a lot, I just never knew what to say. No, that's a lie. I knew what to say but I couldn't bring myself to actually say it," I said. I wanted him to understand how hard it was for me, how scared I was to say or do anything that wasn't answering simple questions.

He smiled broadly, saying, "I'm just really proud of you that you took that huge step and tried to find yourself. And I'll be here now, for when it gets scary. We'll help each other out, alright?"

I nodded. "Alright."

A promise. And one I vowed I wouldn't break.

11

The smile on my face was sky-high. It seemed impossible to even try to lessen the joy radiating off me — and I didn't want to try. The light, fluttering happiness was so beautifully euphoric I never wanted it to end.

My parents had been constantly looking at me when I was texting George and I could feel their piercing eyes boring into me, but I ignored them. They probably suspected something, but I didn't care. They hadn't said anything so I wasn't going to worry until they did – if they did at all. I knew I should've been more concerned, and I should have been hiding this overwhelming joy from them because I knew they wouldn't be happy with me having a boyfriend, and I didn't want them to ruin this. But I couldn't help myself, and I couldn't bring myself to care.

George had taken the step to ask me to be his girlfriend. I said yes, of course. I supposed he'd overcome his fear that we were moving too fast, or he wanted to prove to me that he was serious about us. But maybe he really was ready for making it more official, wanting to go forward. But, whatever the reason, I trusted he meant it. And I knew I wanted us to be together.

But we hadn't really made it public yet. At least, friends knew, and we didn't hide it at school, but we also didn't publicise it. It wasn't anyone else's business.

Maybe we just weren't quite ready for telling everyone yet. It hadn't even been three weeks yet since we told each other how we felt, and it was already clear George was scared of going too fast. And, if I was being honest, I was too.

I'd never been with anyone before, not even a little bit, and I had no idea how everything was supposed to work. It was all new to me, and I didn't know what to expect or how we were supposed to go about these things. We hadn't been given a handbook but I felt it was something we were just expected to know. And I didn't know what to do with that.

But, in all that uncertainty, I did know this: I didn't want to lose him. I didn't want this happiness to end. And I knew I wanted to get to know him better, share what we're thinking and share our worries and doubts and be there for each other. I knew I wanted to be with him, whatever that meant.

•••

I felt guilty, though, for not telling my parents. I didn't tell them everything anyway, we didn't have that sort of relationship, but I felt it was only fair to tell them I was with someone. But I was worried they'd tell me we'd have to break up, or that they'd somehow ruin what we had.

But, they'd never told me I couldn't have a boyfriend. And I never asked. It never really came up.

I texted George, in my break from revising for the year 11 mocks in December, and asked how his parents took it, as I knew he'd already told them.

George: They gave me a "be careful" speech and they tease me about how happy I am, but they're happy for me, I think.

Zoe: Aha, I'm going to tell my parents now, wish me luck.

George: Good luck! Xxx

And, with that, I walked downstairs, swallowing my fear, and asked my parents if I could talk to them. They both turned to look at me, spinning their chairs and putting down their work, while I stood in front of them in their office.

"What is it, Zoe?" My mum asked.

"I, um. I have a boyfriend," I said, looking at the wall between them.

My parents looked at each other and smiled. "Yeah, we know," my dad said carefully.

My jaw dropped a little in shock.

"Well, we suspected, at least. You've been much happier, texting and talking on the phone much more than usual. We were just waiting for you to tell us," my mum explained.

I felt a bit stupid for not thinking they'd figure it out.

"His name's George," I volunteered.

They both nodded.

"How long?" My dad asked.

I swallowed. I didn't want to lie, but if I told them the truth, they'd be annoyed I hadn't told them earlier. But I had to risk it. "Just over two weeks," I said shyly.

"You should have told us sooner," my mum said, disappointed. I wasn't surprised.

"I know. I'm sorry," I said, knowing it's what they wanted to hear. Leaving out the fact I was scared. That I knew I couldn't really talk to them like I wanted to. How I thought they wouldn't be supportive, which was why I never really told them anything important.

I could see my mum trying to decide whether she wanted to be angrier with me or if she'd let it slide. It could easily have gone either way. Finally, she nodded, accepting my apology.

Huh, I thought, I was expecting to put up more of a fight. Not that I was complaining.

I didn't know what else to say, and, apparently, neither did my parents. They glanced between each other and my dad cleared his throat uncomfortably.

"Well, um. That's it," I stammered, suddenly desperate to get away from their prying eyes.

They both nodded again. My mum said, "Alright. Well, uh, just. Be careful, ok?" She looked as awkward as I felt.

I nodded, feeling a blush rise to my cheeks. "Thanks," I mumbled, not really sure why I was saying it. I turned away and started walking out of the room, continuing when neither of them said anything about it.

I was somewhat shocked that it'd been so easy; I wasn't expecting such a painless event, but I was relieved it had been so simple.

I picked up my phone and typed out a message to George:

Zoe: The luck worked; they were totally fine with it. They didn't really say anything at all.

His reply came only a couple of minutes later.

George: Yay!! Now we're even allowed to be together!!!

His excessive use of exclamation marks made me laugh.

And, seeing his excitement, my worries about my lack of experience evaporated away, and I didn't care that this was all new and scary. Because I knew I had George, and I knew we'd find our way through together.

12

"Zoe, wait up!" a voice shouted behind me. I stopped walking and turned around, seeing George jogging up to me. A smile broke out onto my face at the sight of him. Emily nudged me playfully, a smile on her face too.

We were outside, walking to our tutor room, but stopping for George to catch up. When he came over, he gave me a hug, wrapping his arms around me in a way which made my heart melt. I hugged him back, but stepped away far too quickly, remembering Emily standing next to us. But she didn't seem to mind, considering she was stood there smiling at us.

"Hey," he said, a smile still lighting up his face. He reached for my hand, giving it a squeeze, and we made our way over to the picnic benches.

"Hey," I said. Emily said hi too.

"You alright?" George asked. And I knew he wasn't asking it in that conversational way that everyone did, where they didn't really want to know the answer, they just wanted a response like: "Yeah, good thanks, you?" George actually wanted to know how I was, and that alone made me happier than I was already.

"Yes. Extremely," I said, beaming up at him.

"Emily?" George asked, turning to her.

"I'm good," she said. But she wasn't really paying attention. She was looking at her phone, a smile playing at her lips. I nudged her and she looked up, a smile now covering her face.

She'd started talking to Anna last week, and she'd found out Anna was gay, too. They'd been talking a lot, and on the bus that morning, Emily had asked Anna if they could meet before school started. I guessed the answer was yes.

"Hey, is it alright if I go meet someone and leave you to it?" Emily asked. She looked nervous, but also excited and I felt excited for her. I really hoped this turned out well.

"Of course," George said. I let go of his hand, then went over and hugged Emily.

"You got this," I whispered, hopefully quietly enough so George didn't hear.

"Here goes nothing," she whispered.

We pulled apart, and I gave her arm a squeeze before she started walking away.

"Good luck," I called, and she turned to look at me over her shoulder, giving me a smile. I watched her walk away, and she had a light spring in her step. I knew how much she wanted this.

"Who's she meeting?" George asked as we started walking again.

"Someone," I said vaguely. I didn't want to lie to George, but it wasn't my place to say. Emily hadn't come out to him yet, and I didn't know if Anna was out, and I wasn't going to ruin it for either of them.

He nodded but didn't push it, understanding not the specifics, but getting the gist anyway. We slid into seats beside each other on the bench, dropping our bags under the table as I twisted to face him.

"So, I was thinking," George said.

"Yes?" I prompted when he didn't continue.

"I want to try and help you be more confident. I'm not sure if there's anything I can do, but I want to help, and I want to at least try. You shouldn't have to live scared of being yourself or hiding behind anything." He took my hand and squeezed it, and a smile crept onto my face.

I didn't know what to say. My heart swelled. I couldn't remember the last time someone had been so determined to try and help me get better. I felt tears brim in my eyes, and I blinked them back. I didn't want to cry now; I was happy.

"Also," he continued. "You're cute when you're confident. Even cuter than normal, anyway."

I laughed, and I leant forward and wrapped my arms around him, resting my head on his shoulder. "Thank you," I whispered. It didn't sound nearly enough for what I felt, but I didn't know what else I could say.

I pulled back, aware that we were in quite a public place within the school. I didn't want to be one of those couples who couldn't keep their hands off each other and made everyone else cringe and I figured George wouldn't want that either.

"You've got trampolining tomorrow tonight, haven't you?" George asked.

"Yup," I said, nodding my head.

"Do you want to do something afterwards?"

I wanted to say yes straight away, but I knew I'd have to ask my mum and I didn't want to make a fuss. "What did you have in mind?" I said instead.

"We could walk down to the park and get a drink maybe, or just hang out?" He seemed slightly nervous. I smiled at him.

"I like that idea. Let me ask my mum," I said. We discussed timings and logistics, and I texted my mum about it, crossing my fingers in the hope she'd let me.

She texted back almost immediately — which was rare for her — and I smiled brightly. "We're good."

"Great, I'll meet you outside the sports hall afterwards." He was beaming, too.

I looked down at my watch and almost startled at the time. Where did that time go? "We need to go, we've only got a couple of minutes before tutor," I said.

We got up and walked to our tutor rooms, talking about what was happening that day. When we arrived at his room, we stood to the side of the corridor and hugged, and I hurried to my tutor room, sliding through the door with only a couple of seconds to spare.

Emily was already at our table, and she looked up when I slid in the seat beside her. She was already smiling.

"So?" I said, drawing out the word, as the teacher walked in. But he didn't ask for silence, so I pretended he wasn't there. I raised my eyebrows at her.

"I can't stop smiling, it's insane," Emily said.

"What happened?" I was smiling too. I was happy for her, so happy.

"We talked a little bit and then, get this, she just asked if I could be her girlfriend! I didn't even have to ask her, she asked me. I said yes, of course. And we're meeting up after school too." She was talking quickly, her voice animated despite the low volume so other people couldn't hear.

72

I gave a little squeal. "That's amazing, I'm so happy for you." I gave her a hug.

We were told to be silent then, for the register, so we both reluctantly stopped talking. But as soon as we were left to our own devices, we carried on.

"We haven't talked about how it's going to work yet, as neither of us are technically out, but we'll figure it out. We'll make something work."

"Of course you will, you're brilliant," I said. I wasn't joking, either. I was immensely grateful to have her as a friend, and she deserved happiness.

We talked for the rest of tutor, ignoring the revision we definitely should have been doing, but I didn't care. It felt so good to just talk and laugh, and I wondered for the hundredth time why I ever thought being alone was better than this.

13

I hurriedly walked down to the PE department, as I was let out late from maths, and changed into my kit as quickly as I could. It was the first session of this year's trampolining club and I didn't want to be late. Normally clubs started at the beginning of term in September, but somehow the trampolining club wasn't organised in time, so we had to wait until after half term, at the beginning of November. I didn't see anyone else in my year, but I recognised a few of the girls in the year below who did it last year too, and I smiled at them. I was shocked, momentarily. Because I didn't even think about it. It seemed these things were starting to come more naturally now.

I had done trampolining after school for the past three years, and luckily, it was the same instructor as always, Lauren. She let us all work at our own level, and she used to teach me complex flips and twists, linking them into extravagant routines. I hoped we'd continue where we left off from last time.

I wanted to join a proper club so I could compete, but my parents said it was too awkward to drive me around all the time. And, if I was honest, I didn't mind so much. I think the extra pressure and worry may have been too much for me anyway.

I made my way down to the hall alone, and despite being late, I was still one of the first down. The familiar sight of the blue edges, the white bed and the metal framework of the folded trampolines, ready to be set up, set my mind at ease and I no longer worried about how it might turn out. Just knowing I'd have the exhilarating feeling of trampolining again was enough to calm me.

Lauren was talking with Kim, the other instructor, but when she saw me, she smiled and finished her conversation, and walked over to me. I smiled brightly at her, with her light blue eyes and dark brown, almost black, hair that fell perfectly around her face in large ringlets.

"Zoe," she said warmly, giving me a hug. "How are you?"

"Hey, Lauren. I'm — I'm good," I said. And I meant in. I really was good. I felt happy there. Even when I was trying to be invisible, I wasn't there. After the first term, I became comfortable with the people at the club. They were all kind and easy to be around and I could relax with them in a way I hadn't thought possible. I wasn't close to any of them; we never talked beyond the walls of the sports hall. But I wasn't too bothered by it.

"I'm glad to hear that. How's school going?"

I didn't think she was talking about school, not really. I thought she was referring to my lack of friends and lack of confidence, which I had told her about last year. I'd stayed behind to help her pack up one night, delaying the inevitable of having to go home and drown in my thoughts. I remembered how suddenly I broke down, right there in front of her. She took it in her stride, being the comfort I so desperately needed. She'd been so kind about it all, not treating me any differently, as I'd feared.

"It's better. Really great, actually," I said, smiling to myself at the thought of George and Emily.

"That's amazing to hear, Zoe. I'm happy for you." She gave my arm a gentle squeeze and smiled. I couldn't help but feel happy too, a warm fuzz spreading through me.

"And I'm working at becoming less invisible. Like, putting myself out there a bit more and trying to gain some confidence. Working on what I was struggling with before," I said, overcome with a sudden surge of confidence. I didn't care that I was vulnerable in that moment because I trusted Lauren and I knew she understood.

"I'm really proud of you. That's a big step," she said. "Remember, I'm here if you ever want to talk."

I nodded. "Thank you," I said, with a smile.

We continued chatting for the next few minutes while the others came in. I'd almost forgotten how friendly and kind Lauren was, how easy it was to talk to her. I'd missed these sessions more than I realised, and I hadn't even started on the trampolines yet.

There were two separate groups, with an instructor for each, and eight people in each group. There were only seven in my group so far, but Lauren seemed unconcerned about that.

I was glad I'd gotten Lauren as an instructor again. She was much kinder than Kim, and she explained moves better. I was glad, again, that we kept the same instructor throughout the year, too.

Lauren asked each of our names, quite unnecessarily as all but two of us were together in previous years, but we complied anyway.

"Zoe," I said, chin up when the small circle we'd created around Lauren came around to my turn, I smiled, comforted by the familiar faces around me. This wasn't nearly as bad as I was imagining.

I inwardly scolded myself for worrying about it all so much beforehand, when I knew it would be alright. I knew these people, and Lauren was so sweet and kind to me, to all of us. I loved trampolining, and I hated how I let my anxiety get the better of me at times like this. But the gnawing in my stomach was ebbing away as I realised I was going to enjoy the next hour and a half, and nothing bad was going to happen.

The door banged open behind me, and we all twisted to see who had come in. It was a boy in my year who I vaguely recognised, an echo of familiarity.

He walked over, and said, "Sorry I'm late," his voice shaking and breathing heavily. Lauren sighed but didn't say anything about his lateness. She then went over all the safety, which I'd heard about a million times before. It was like on a plane, where you knew what was being said but you knew you should listen anyway. But then half tuned out at the familiar words despite yourself.

I glanced over at the boy, trying to be subtle about it but failing considerably. He was looking at me too, but quickly looked away as soon as our eyes met. I was sure I recognised him from somewhere, but I couldn't figure out where exactly.

His hair, a dirty blond colour, was cropped short, close to his head. His eyes were a deep green, with short lashes lining them. He looked up at me, and instead of flicking his gaze away again, he smiled awkwardly.

Then it clicked.

My primary school had a connection to another one close by, and we were given pen-pals, of a sort, from the other school. We called them buddies. We talked over email and wrote letters too, once our handwriting was good enough and we'd earned our pen license. My buddy was the boy, hurrying in late: Zack.

We talked a lot, from year three when we were assigned the buddies up until year six at the end of primary school. We'd met up a lot, in and outside of the school buddy system, where our parents would arrange for us to go to each other's houses. But as he got older, he became more and more rude and unkind and the time we spent together was no longer enjoyable. At the end of year six, the last time we met up, Zack said he had a crush on me, but when I told him I wasn't interested, he turned angry and even more rude. I was scared, the fire in his eyes no longer because of passion and I feared what he might do.

Maybe it was irrational and unfair, but we didn't speak after that. He didn't get in contact, and neither did I. I knew he went to my school, but we'd never crossed paths. And now almost five years had passed and we were in close proximity for the first time since then.

I could tell he wasn't comfortable being in the same room as me. He awkwardly scratched his head when I looked at him, even out of the corner of my eye, and his eyes flittered around as if trying to focus on something other than me, but failing to do so.

Once Lauren finished telling us all the rules and safety, we headed over to the trampolines on the other side of the room, working together smoothly to put them up, almost all our movements practised. There were two trampolines and four people to each trampoline, and I walked over to one at random. I hoped Zack would choose the other, but he walked up to my side to join me. I inwardly groaned.

"Hey!" Zack said, too happily. His voice was deeper than before, almost a low rumble.

"Hi," I said, my voice expressionless. It sounded as if I was bored, but I was far from that. I had to fight to keep my voice from shaking. I didn't want to let him get close, didn't want to give him the chance to hurt me again. It's one thing opening yourself up to people, but it's another to let someone who's already hurt you do it again.

"You've changed a bit." There was a slightly mocking tone to his voice and I couldn't think of anything to say.

I didn't want to be mean to him. I really didn't. It happened a long time ago, and everyone deserved a second chance. But I remembered clearly how upset I had been that his behaviour had changed so suddenly and I'd lost one of my childhood friends at the flick of a switch.

"Yeah, well. I've grown up," I said finally.

Zack huffed but didn't reply.

He'd changed a lot, too. His features were less childlike, and his hair was shorter and more sophisticated than it was five years ago. He wasn't much taller — he was tall for his age when we were friends — but he'd lost the awkwardness surrounding that.

We established the order, and Lauren told me to go first for the warm-up, so I jumped up, pulling my legs up behind me. It didn't matter that I hadn't been on a trampoline for a few months, I immediately fell into the rhythm of jumping, lifting my arms up above my head as I jumped up, and bringing them down as I came down, bending my knees on impact and pushing off again, gaining height on each jump.

It all came naturally to me – like I was made to jump and twist my body in the air in the time before I landed again. I loved how I could be in the air for seconds at a time, tucking my legs up or straightening them out in front of me, feeling in control and weightless. Like if I only jumped a little higher I could reach the sky; I could fly away and leave my problems behind.

But I could see Zack out of the corner of my eye, just standing there looking me up and down as if he were examining me. It made my skin prickle, but I tried to ignore him.

I jumped down once I'd finished, and Zack smiled at me, less awkwardly now. "You're really good," he said, sounding sincere.

I looked at him for a moment, trying to hide my shock. "Thanks."

"Have you been doing this long?" Zack asked. I couldn't tell if he was genuinely interested or if he was just making conversation.

"This will be my fourth year," I said.

He nodded. "Look, I'm sorry. For what happened. I shouldn't have acted how I did. I know I should have said this a lot sooner, so I'm sorry for that too," Zack said.

I didn't say anything at first. I didn't look at him either, I couldn't. Because I wanted to forgive him. That would be the right thing to do and I wanted to do the right thing. But it was five years late, and I'd long forgotten about it all, so what difference would it make?

I must have waited too long to reply because Zack carried on before I'd had a chance to say anything. "I'm not asking for anything, I swear. It's way too late to save our friendship, but I hope it isn't too late to ask for forgiveness."

I smiled at him, a small smile which barely lifted the corners of my lips. I thought about how much courage that must have taken him, to say all that, with other people listening around us. I thought how hard it was for me to do anything out of my comfort zone and how much willpower it took. And suddenly I felt the old grudge slip away, like water running to the ocean.

"Ok," I started, nodding my head. "I forgive you."

His face broke into a wide smile, the relief evident in his eyes. I couldn't help but smile wider too.

"Thank you, I really appreciate that."

I nodded again.

"Zack, your turn," Lauren said. Zack looked slightly panicked, and I realised he probably hadn't been on a trampoline before.

"It's ok, you'll be great. It's really fun," I said, giving him a small push towards the trampoline, urging him forward. He looked back at me, still with the worry in his eyes, but I nodded my head towards the trampoline again and he walked up to it.

I watched as he pulled himself up, somewhat awkwardly, seeming like he had too many limbs, and I had to resist the urge to laugh a little.

"I'll talk you through it," I said, looking at Lauren for permission.

She nodded, a smile playing at her lips. "Go ahead. You're as good as I am at this bit."

I smiled brightly, pride blooming within me, before turning back to Zack. I talked him through what to do with his arms and legs, in the same way Lauren had with me all those years ago. I gave little tips, how to gain more height or to make transitions easier and I saw how his unsteady and trembling legs slowly began to steady a little.

"Old friend?" Lauren asked, raising her eyebrow at me.

"Of a sort. We're friends again now, I think." And I hoped I was right. Because although we couldn't get back what we had was lost, maybe we would be able to make something else, something different.

Lauren nodded and smiled, but didn't say anything else. I went back to help Zack.

I was glad I'd forgiven him. It didn't change what had happened, but I believed we'd be able to move on and not having the awkward tension between us would make the hours spent in the hall much more enjoyable. Not just for us, but for everyone.

It would make the banter and the rallying of conversations more relaxed and easy. And that was one of the things I loved most about the club and the community we created. It didn't matter that I barely knew anything about any of the others, we just got on and we had plenty to laugh and joke about. That easy-going friendship was one of the only things which kept me afloat when I was drowning, and though I didn't need that lifeboat so much with George and Emily in the picture; it was still a comfort which I would have been reluctant to give up.

14

George was already standing outside the sports hall doors once trampolining had finished, and he smiled when he spotted me looking at him as we were packing away. I gestured for him to come inside, and he opened the door and stepped in.

The younger students had already left, and it was just me, Zack and another girl called Megan in the year below helping Lauren fold up the trampolines.

"Hey," I called over. "I won't be long."

"It's cool, don't worry," he said, eyeing the trampoline still set up with a strange kind of confusion in his eyes.

Lauren raised her eyebrows at me, and I couldn't help but laugh. "Lauren, this is George. My boyfriend," I said, smiling. It felt nice, those words on my lips.

"Hey," he said, nodding his head in her direction.

"Is this who you were referencing earlier?" Lauren asked me. I nodded. "Nice to meet you, George," she said, turning to him.

"You, too," he said politely.

"Zoe, you can go now, if you want," Lauren said.

"Oh, it's ok. I don't mind," I said, hating being unhelpful.

"Really, you always help. Have a day off." She looked me in the eyes, a smile playing at her lips.

"Alright. Thank you, Lauren." She nodded.

I said bye to Zack and Megan and picked up my stuff, walking over to George who gave me a quick hug. We walked out and he reached for my hand, interweaving our fingers together. We talked as we walked through the school, down the drive and towards the park, and I told him about trampolining and what had happened with Zack that day, and all the years before it. It was nice to be able to talk about Zack with someone. I barely spoke about it at the time, and it was nice to finally be able to voice my thoughts with someone who I knew cared about me and my feelings. And George listened.

I felt like maybe I didn't have to go through every single thing alone, and maybe I could talk about whatever I was feeling or thinking without the whole world crashing down around me. I realised that telling someone else your worries didn't burden them: that wasn't how it worked. Telling someone only reduced your burden.

Worries weren't like energy — worries could be destroyed. Telling someone else didn't transfer the worry to them, it sent the thoughts to the wind, where the air could reduce them to dust, if you let it.

•••

"How are you liking life now you're not hiding inside yourself?" George asked. We were sat outside the café next to the park, enjoying the unusually warm day, for early November. I had a mug of hot chocolate on the table in front of me, while George had a coffee.

"Way better than life before," I said. I looked out at the trees in the park, the huge bushes and the shabby children's play area, which consisted of only a slide and one lonely swing. I sipped my hot chocolate. "It's like I've stepped into the real world and I can finally be a part of it, instead of watching from a distance. And I wouldn't be friends with Emily if I hadn't done this, so even if that was the only thing I gained, it would have been worth it, for her."

As I said it, I realised how true it was. All the other stuff was great, too, but if I only found Emily in this experiment of mine, I would have been happy. All the rest was simply a bonus.

George nodded as if he understood. "I'm glad, too. I'm glad to be friends with her and I'm happy for you."

"Thanks," I said, reaching across the table to take his hand in mine. He squeezed, and I squeezed back, smiling up at him as I took another sip of my drink, the hot liquid burning on the way down.

We chatted for a while longer as we both finished our drinks, about music and books and other small things, which made me feel as though I was becoming closer to him, even though I hardly learnt anything new.

Once we'd finished, we left and walked to the park, hand in hand, where we carried on walking around the weaving path. This park wasn't as nice as the one where we'd met up in half term, closer to our houses, but this one was only a five-minute walk from school, so it was much more practical for after school. It was still nice, though, if you avoided the forest part where people from school got drunk and wasted. We stayed clear of that part, sticking to the well-lit area as the sun starting setting.

We walked, talking about whatever came to mind, until just before our parents were due to pick us up, where we circled back to the car park to wait. We sat on the bench which was by the square of tarmac, and we barely left a millimetre gap between our bodies. I didn't want to leave George. I wanted to stay next to him, with his arm around me and my head resting on his shoulder, where I felt safe and loved.

I glanced up at him, twisting my head to look at his face. He looked down at me too, and our eyes locked. We just looked at each other for a minute, and suddenly I wanted to lean up and press my lips to his.

I wasn't thinking about the fact that it would be my first kiss or how that might have been going too fast. Because it felt right. I wanted to kiss him then, sitting on that hard and rickety bench with the wind whipping my hair around my head. I stretched my neck up, my eyes on his full lips, and he bent his head down, and we were so close, our lips almost touching. It would have only taken a tiny movement to close that gap.

But I heard a car engine slowing down and I jumped back, suddenly remembering where we were and how my mum was about to pick me up. I saw a car round the corner, and I recognised the black metal immediately. My heart was pounding. She can't have seen us; trees were hiding us from view. But she could see us now, and I had to fight the urge to shuffle further away from George.

I attempted to steady my breathing, and I could tell George was doing the same. "I'm so, so sorry," I said.

The moment had passed, and I didn't want my first kiss to be in front of my mum, anyway. I felt oddly angry at her for showing up at just that moment. But of course it wasn't her fault, and I drowned the fire before it could really take hold.

"It's ok," George said, giving my hand a squeeze. I nodded.

My mum was parking, and I made to stand up when she opened the car door, stepped out and locked it behind her. Oh no, I thought. She was coming over. I stood up anyway, and so did George, clearly sensing what was about to unfold.

"I'm sorry," I whispered again.

But George didn't have time to reply, because my mum was walking up to us now, a smile on her face. I couldn't tell if she was faking it or not.

"Hello, there," my mum said. I cringed inwardly.

"Hi, mum. Mum, this is George. George, this is my mum, Molly," I said, gesturing to each pathetically, unnecessarily. I felt on edge and I tried hard to hide it.

"Hello, Molly," George said, sticking out his hand for her to shake, which she did.

"Nice to meet you, George," my mum said, all smiles.

"You too." He seemed so at ease, taking it all in his stride.

"Did you two have a nice time?" My mum asked.

"Yes, thank you. Your daughter is lovely company," George said, smiling down at me. I smiled back. He was being so polite, and I suppressed a laugh at how old fashioned he sounded, but somehow it suited him.

"Good, good," my mum said. "Well, it was lovely to meet you, George, but we best be going. Are your parents here yet?" she asked.

George looked around the car park, and just then a car pulled in. "Yeah, my mum's just here now," he said, nodding in the direction of the car.

My mum nodded, and we all walked to the car park together. George and I walked behind my mum, and as we got to the car, I gave George a hug and promised to call him later that evening, saying goodbye. I watched him walk over, and he pulled the door open and the woman in the driver's seat waved and smiled at me, but didn't get out. I was secretly glad. I could barely see her, just a flicker of auburn brown hair through the open door before I realised my mum was tapping her fingers impatiently on the steering wheel, and I fumbled to open my door.

"Sorry," I mumbled, as I slid in and clicked my seat belt in place. She reversed out of the parking space, and as we passed George's car, I caught a better look at his mum. Both my mum and I glanced over.

I still couldn't catch much, because George was smiling at me and I couldn't bring myself to pull my eyes away from his, and by the time I did, I had to swivel my neck around to see his mum, and that too became too hard.

My mum took a sharp intake of breath and I looked over at her, but her eyes were on the road again. "What?" I asked.

My mum didn't say anything for a moment too long. "Nothing, nothing. She just looks like someone I used to know, that's all."

But I knew that wasn't all. But before I could ask her more about it, she carried on. "He seems nice," she said.

I nodded. "Yeah, he's really nice."

"And you like him?"

I nodded again, even though she probably couldn't see. "Yes. A lot." I felt vaguely uncomfortable talking about it with her, but luckily she didn't press any more, and I resorted to looking out the window, thinking of all that happened that day and trying not to think about the fact that my mum was clearly lying to me.

15

"Emily?" I said. We were on the floor of my room, me lying on the floor and Emily leant against my bed. I was sketching, a messy drawing of a lotus flower for my school art project, and Emily was writing a practice essay for English — which I'd have to do later that night.

"Mmm?" Emily said, looking up from her work.

I pulled myself up so I was sitting too, and I folded my legs beneath me. "How are things going with Anna?"

It was a few days after they'd become an item — officially but not publicly yet — and Emily had been all smiles, but hadn't told me much. Which was fine, of course she could have her own girlfriend without telling me everything, but I was starting to become curious.

"Really good. We've been talking almost non-stop and we met up again after school. It was amazing. I really, really like her. Like, so much it's scary." Emily sounded flustered, but in a good way.

"That's how it should be," I said.

"Maybe."

"So, when can I meet her?" I asked.

"You already have!" She laughed.

Technically, this was true. I had talked to Anna before. We were in the same art class for the past year and she was in my German too; I knew her enough to know she was lovely. But I hadn't met her yet as Emily's girlfriend, and that was what I was getting at. I said as much to Emily.

"Well, er," she said, suddenly looking sheepish and serious. "I maybe sort of invited her to have lunch with us tomorrow."

I couldn't help but squeal. "Yay! That's great, I can't wait."

"The thing is, George still doesn't know. I don't want to exclude him, but I also think it might be easier if he wasn't there. For Anna too. I told her that you knew about us and that you were cool and she seemed ok with that, but I don't want to put too much on her, you know?" Emily paused and took a breath as if the next part was harder. "She's still trying to figure some stuff out and I completely understand how hard that is. So I think maybe George shouldn't be there. Sorry."

I almost wanted to laugh, because she seemed so worried for no reason at all. "Don't apologise. George won't care that he doesn't eat lunch with us once. He, unlike us, has other friends." We both laughed. "Do you want me to talk to him for you?"

Emily shook her head. "No, I don't think so. Maybe we could talk to him at break tomorrow though. Or maybe before school. I'll come out to him, and explain about Anna. He'll be cool, won't he?"

"Yeah, definitely. You sure about telling him, though?"

"Yes. I want him to know." She accompanied this with a vigorous nod.

"Alright. Before school?" She nodded. "I'll text him to make sure he's there and we'll meet at the picnic benches and talk, ok?" She nodded again.

I messaged George, being vague enough to not release anything but making the importance of it obvious. I told him not to worry, too, hoping that was enough.

"I'll be there with you. You'll have me," I said, and went over to hug her. "Plus, I know I already like Anna so that's a bonus."

She laughed, and I could almost feel the tension seep out of her.

•••

The next day at school, Emily was practically bouncing on her heels, in anticipation and worry, I assumed.

"Hey, it's going to be ok," I said, putting my hand on her arm which stopped the bouncing.

"Yeah. Yeah. It's going to be fine."

And before she could say that to herself again and again like I knew she was in her head, George came into view and he was beside us in no time. He gave me a quick hug, then turned serious.

"Hey, what's up?" He said. He did look slightly concerned, and I hoped I hadn't worried him.

I glanced at Emily. She took a deep breath, closed her eyes for a moment, then spoke, launching right in. "George, I'm gay."

He smiled. A wide, sincere smile. "That's cool," he said. And I released a breath I hadn't realised I'd been holding.

Emily broke into a smile and I saw her visibly relax. I grinned at her and nodded my head a little to urge her to continue.

"And I have a girlfriend." She looked a little sheepish now.

"That's great! I'm really happy for you, Emily. I really am," George said.

"Thanks. Um, would you mind if you didn't sit with us at lunch today? I want you guys to meet her but I don't want to overwhelm her. I just think it'd be better, for today, if it was just Zoe. Sorry, George," Emily said.

"Of course, I don't mind. Honestly, I understand, don't worry about it," George said. He smiled at her and I felt so relieved for Emily.

We chatted until it was time to go to tutor, and Emily filled George in on what's been going on with Anna. When we got up to leave, George gave Emily a hug, saying, "I'm here for you. It'll be ok."

And my feelings for George suddenly intensified, if that was even possible, to see him so supportive of Emily, and I couldn't help but believe him that it was all going to be ok.

"Are you ok?" I asked Emily when George had gone to his tutor room.

"Yeah. I really am." And I knew she meant it.

•••

I tapped my fingers absentmindedly on the table in front of me as I waited for Emily to come to meet me with Anna. I felt oddly nervous, and I couldn't imagine how Emily and Anna must have been feeling.

After what seemed like an eternity — but was actually barely one minute after I sat down — I saw Emily walking towards me, with Anna by her side. They were talking, both of them smiling, and I couldn't help but smile too. They both looked so happy, heart-warmingly so.

"Hey," I said, smiling still, and turning to Anna. "How are you?"

"Hi. I'm really good, thanks," Anna said, smiling too. They both sat down, across from me, with Emily in her usual seat and Anna next to her. I imagined how this may become a common occurrence, the four of us becoming friends. Just the thought of it made me smile even wider.

"How's your day been so far?" I asked. Emily and I pulled out our lunch boxes, and Anna seemed to take this as a signal to get her own out, too.

"Alright," both Emily and Anna said at the same time, and we all laughed. And with the laughter, some of the awkward tension dissipated and it was easier to talk after that.

I got to know Anna better, and we talked about hobbies and music and small things like that, and we got on well. I decided I liked her a lot, and I was even more happy for Emily after seeing how lovely Anna clearly was. We laughed and joked and talked, and I noticed Emily stealing glances at Anna, with nothing but care in her eyes.

But, we didn't talk about the two of them together, despite the fact we all knew. We didn't mention anything about what Anna was trying to figure out, and I could tell she was relieved. When the end of lunch came around, far too soon, we all stood up reluctantly and I gave both Emily and Anna a hug, hoping again to get the message across that I really was ok with them being together and with whoever Anna became.

"I hope I'll be seeing more of you," I said to Anna, smiling.

She beamed and nodded. "Yeah, me too." She glanced over at Emily again, and she smiled even wider, if that was possible.

We all turned in opposite directions to go to our next lesson, and as I was walking, I thought about how proud of Emily I was, that she was going for what made her happy despite the hell she may have had to face. And I thought how hard it may be for her and I made a silent vow to myself to try and make it easier for her if I could.

16

When trampolining finished the next week, I started to head to the music practice rooms where George would be practising with his band. I still had forty-five minutes until my mum picked me up — normally I wouldn't have had to wait so long, but she had a meeting so she couldn't get me any earlier, and we only had the one car. There wasn't a bus I could get either as there wasn't a late bus which went in the direction of my house. But I didn't mind, I could surprise George and take him up on his offer from all those weeks ago.

I was rounding the corner to where the music suits were when I heard quick footsteps behind me. I stopped and turned around, but no one was there. I assumed I must have mistaken the beat of a drum for footsteps.

But despite the logical reasonings, my heart rate picked up and I felt the familiar grasp of panic starting to take hold. I tried to swallow it down, but the fact that most people had already left the school — I'd stayed behind to talk to Lauren, leaving everyone else to leave before me and most clubs let out earlier than trampolining anyway — left me oddly unnerved, in a way it didn't normally.

I carried on walking but I barely managed a few steps before I was shoved against the wall. My back hit the wall, hard, and pain shot through me, but I ignored it. I bit down a yelp, not wanting to attract attention until I'd grasped the situation better.

It was a boy, who I thought must have been in my year, though I'd only ever seen him once or twice previously and I didn't know who he was. I assumed he must have been new. His hair was long, lying flat against his head and hanging lifelessly around his shoulders. He wasn't much taller than I was, but he held an air of intimidation which fuelled the rising panic within me. He had my body pinned to the wall, his hands gripping my wrists and holding them to the side of me while he stood in front of me, and I was acutely aware of how he'd cornered me, making it impossible to escape.

I couldn't even start to fathom what I'd done to warrant this. He still hadn't said anything, and I wracked my brain for anything I may have done to enrage him so much, but came up empty.

He whipped his head around, checking that still, no one had come. His eyes shifted to me, examining me. I felt naked, like he could see right through my clothes, and even farther than that to what lies beneath the surface. His gaze never really rested anywhere. After he scanned me from head to toe and back again, again, again, his eyes rested on mine, making me feel even more exposed than before. I resisted the urge to squirm beneath his steel grip.

He breathed in like he was about to say something, but he closed his mouth again and continued to stare at me. I didn't know what to do. Should I have said something? Or just return his stare? Neither of us spoke and the only thing that filled the silence was my fast, uneven breaths and his slow, steady ones. How could he be so calm? I tried to steady my breathing to appear calmer, but that only seemed to make it faster. Everything wasn't going to be alright. Something was going to happen and I didn't know what that was and there was nothing I could do about it. And nothing I did seemed to lessen that panic.

My throat tightened and I suddenly felt overheated, overwhelmed. No, I thought, this can't be happening now. I tried to swallow down the panic attack which threatened to consume me.

I could feel the low, distant rumble of a bass line, feel the vibration of the floor beneath me and the wall behind me more than hear the sound it created. I reminded myself that music, that beat, the pulsing heartbeat of the building, was coming from George and his band and, though it did little to calm me, I felt less overwhelmed and I felt it wouldn't be impossible to get through this.

I wanted to scream out, knowing if I yelled loud enough they'd hear me over their music, but I was more terrified of what this boy could do to me if I brought attention to myself, so I kept quiet, despite the desperate need to ask for help.

"What do you want?" Somehow I plucked up the courage to say something. Surprisingly, my voice sounded relatively confident and even, despite the rocks stuck in my throat, making it difficult to pull oxygen into my body.

"What I want is for you to stop stealing what's mine," he said. His voice was low and intimidating, almost a growl which made me involuntarily shrink away from him, pressing my body even harder into the solid wall behind me. I thought, distantly, how he looked like one of my drawings I'd done the week before, all raw emotion and anger etched onto his features.

I furrowed my eyebrows slightly because I had no idea what he was talking about.

"I'm sorry, what?" I asked. It was easier to speak now, the tightness having subsided a little, probably from the confusion of the moment.

He huffed, loudly, and I felt his warm breath on my face. I tried not to gag.

"I should be in your position. I should get the happy family. I should at least be a goddamn part of it," he said, getting increasingly agitated and angry, breathing hard now. "And you won't even acknowledge me." He wasn't talking loudly, quite the opposite, but the quiet menace in his voice scared me more than his yelling would have.

I felt so utterly confused in that moment. I gathered he had a bad family life, but that didn't explain why he seemed to hold me personally responsible or why he thought he should be a part of my family. As for not acknowledging him? I was even more confused as to why I should have. As far as I knew, he was just another face in the three hundred other people in my year.

"I'm sorry," I said again. "Who are you?"

"I think you know," he said, voice stern and sharp. He was still looking at my face, but his gaze wasn't settled on my eyes anymore.

"I really don't. I swear." I would have been angry if I wasn't so lost in what was happening. The panic was slowly ebbing away as the threat seemed to lessen.

He looked stumped like I was supposed to know who he was. There appeared to be an internal struggle as he decided whether I was telling the truth or not. Whatever he decided, he said, "Robert Cooksley. Rob."

I didn't recognise the name.

I must have looked at Rob blankly, because he asked, "You don't know my name?"

His grip on my wrists loosened. I shook my head. "No, I don't think I've ever heard it before. I swear." I hoped I didn't sound like I was denying it too much and sounding guilty. I really hadn't ever heard the name before.

Rob let go of me and I almost slumped against the wall from the release, but I stayed upright. He stepped back, and I shuffled away from the wall a little so my back wasn't pressed into the rough surface anymore. All his anger seemed to deflate out of him.

"You don't know who I am," he said, almost to himself. I shook my head again, anyway.

"Shit."

I looked at him, completely lost as to what was happening. He was whipping his head around again and he seemed anxious and on edge.

"Is everything ok?" I asked carefully.

He looked at me and he seemed surprised to see me standing there as if he'd forgotten I was there. He didn't answer me. Instead, he said, "I'm sorry. I'm really sorry, Zoe." He sounded pained. I realised, distantly, that I hadn't told him my name.

"What for?"

He shook his head, a continuous movement that lasted a few seconds. "I can't. I'm sorry." He started to back away, stepping away from me, but still facing me.

"I shouldn't have done that. I thought you knew. I'm sorry."

"Knew what?" I was getting worried now: like it was an important piece of information that I was missing.

He carried on walking backwards, small steps, but steps all the same. He shook his head, again, again, again. "I can't be the one to tell you."

"Tell me what?" I was getting annoyed now. Why couldn't he just explain what he meant, rather than talking in riddles? I started walking after him, but that only made him speed up. "Stop, please. Talk to me."

He stopped, at least. But he was still shaking his head. It seemed subconscious by this point. "I can't. It's not my place." He was determined on that, apparently.

"Whose place is it, then?" I asked, but I wasn't sure if I really wanted to know the answer.

He didn't say anything for a moment, and I thought he wasn't going to. But then he spoke. And I wished he hadn't. "Ask your parents."

A heavy dread settled over me. "What?" I furrowed my eyebrows, but I was too stunned to say anything more.

But he'd already turned away and was walking faster now away from me. He spoke over his shoulder, those same words again. "I'm sorry." I wondered what exactly he was sorry for.

Then he started walking faster and faster, almost a run, and he was gone. I contemplated running after him, but my feet were stuck to the ground and my legs had become frozen blocks beneath me.

17

I watched, helplessly, as Rob pushed the doors open and ran through them, breaking into a sprint as he ran away from the building, from me.

And suddenly, unbidden, the bubbling panic started to rise again. I stumbled back, desperate for something to lean against, and my hand made contact with the wall behind me before the rest of my body did. I leaned the back of my head against it, trying to focus on the hard brick beneath the layers of paint. But I couldn't.

I couldn't get those words out of my head: *ask your parents.* What did my parents have to do with this? Have they been keeping something a secret? I couldn't even fathom what it might have been. But that didn't stop my thoughts spiralling out of control as my breathing became ragged.

I slumped down, landing with a dull thud on the floor which probably would have hurt had I been aware of anything. I leant forward with my head between my knees, and I tried again to focus on something other than my racing thoughts, with the racing heartbeat to match. I tried to breathe, counting each one, but it seemed to have no effect and I couldn't concentrate on it enough.

And still, those words circled around my head in an endless stream.

I heard footsteps again, but they seemed far away, and I couldn't bring myself to lift my head. But then they became hurried and I was aware of a voice saying my name. I tried to focus on that.

"Zoe." I recognised his voice. George sounded worried, concerned, his voice twisting and breaking unnaturally in a way which gave me the strength to look up.

He was rushing towards me, running now to cover the distance of the short corridor between us. His eyebrows were knitted together slightly and I heard a soft thud. I looked down and a water bottle rolled on the floor near him, hitting the wall where he must have dropped it, and I couldn't take my eyes off it.

Despite myself, I felt tears rush down my cheeks. Somehow, the sight of that falling water bottle made this all real, and I hadn't dreamt the whole Rob ordeal. Sadness and confusion crashed through me and I didn't know what to do anymore. I carried on staring at the bottle, not having the energy to care about George, bare meters away.

I felt his hands on my shoulders, strong and sure. "Hey, hey," he said, his voice soft and gentle, but somehow stern too.

I didn't look up.

"It's ok. I'm here. You're ok. You're ok." He repeated this again and again, and told me to breathe, in through the nose and out through the mouth. And, finally, finally, I started to breathe more easily, and I looked up at him, a weak smile playing at my lips.

He sat down next to me, not saying anything, and I leant against him gratefully.

"Zoe, what happened?" George asked, his voice gentle, after a few minutes had passed.

I just shook my head. I couldn't talk about it now, not quite yet. I wanted to tell him, but not here, not in the same place where it happened. We were even leaning against the same wall.

"Ok. Do you want to go somewhere else?" He asked.

I nodded. Somehow words seemed too much.

"Come on." He stood up and helped pull me up, taking my hand in his. We walked over to the exit, and we stopped at one of the doors, a music practice room. "I'll be right back, I promise."

I nodded again. He ducked in, and I heard muffled voices through the door. He was back after barely a minute, with a bag slung on his back. I noticed, with a swell of warmth, that he was holding my bag too. I'd completely forgotten about it.

"I can take that," I said, gesturing towards my bag in his hand. He just shook his head, and I didn't have the energy to argue.

I reached for his hand, weaving my fingers through his, needing someone, something, to hold onto. We walked out, hand in hand, side by side, not talking; only the sound of our footsteps and the quiet whistle of the wind filling the silence.

We reached the school gates and walked past them to the low brick wall that everyone used as a bench, ignoring the faded sign banning just that.

"Come on," George said, making his way to the wall and sitting down. I followed him and sat up close to him so there was barely centimetres between us. He dropped both our bags on the floor next to him, and I leant into him, laying my head on his shoulder. I sighed, suddenly feeling overwhelmed again by everything that had happened. I looked at the road a few metres in front of us, watching the few cars drive past. George wrapped his arm around me, pulling me closer to him and his body heat transferred into mine. And, sitting there on the uncomfortable brick wall with George by my side and our fingers locked together, I felt safe, like nothing bad could happen. My breathing returned to normal, and the clawing and grasping panic in my chest and tummy slowly ebbed away.

"You going to tell me what happened?" asked George, his voice serious, breaking the silence.

"Yeah." I hated thinking about what had happened, but I wanted George to know. He deserved to know, and they say talking about these things helps you understand and get over them.

I took a deep breath and lifted my head from his shoulder.

"I was going to surprise you, see you with your band after trampolining. But then he just shoved me and pinned me to the wall and started saying all these crazy things…" I told George what Robert had said and what had happened, not leaving out any details. He listened to every word and I tried to not notice the concern knitted on his forehead. He squeezed my hand from time to time, sometimes so hard it hurt, but it was comforting: I didn't mind.

"Zoe," George said, lost for words. "I wish I could do something to help."

"You being here is enough," I said, smiling. I meant it, too. Just with George by my side, everything suddenly seemed less problematic and less daunting.

Tears prickled in my eyes and I tried to blink them back, but couldn't. One spilt over my eyelids and trickled down my cheek, followed by more, starting a flow which seemed unlikely to stop.

"Sorry," I said, feeling embarrassed about crying over something like this. I wiped my fingertips over my cheeks and under my eyes, angry at them, trying to stop the stream.

"You don't have to be strong with me. It's ok. I won't judge you for crying, ever," George said, his voice filled with love.

He wrapped his other arm around me, strong and sure, and I cried silently into his shirt. I was smaller than him and I felt cocooned in his warm embrace.

When the tears finally stopped, I pulled back from his arms reluctantly.

"What time is it?" I'd forgotten to put my watch back on after trampolining, and I had no idea how much time had passed since I'd left the sports hall.

"Just gone five," George said, after checking his phone for the time. I couldn't believe that everything with Rob had only lasted half an hour — it seemed so much longer than that.

"That's ok, then. We've still got fifteen minutes until my mum picks me up. When are you getting picked up?" I leant back into him, no longer worried about the far-away threat of my mum seeing us huddled together like this.

"Whenever I'm ready. I'll text them later," George said dismissively.

I nodded against his shoulder.

"What are you going to do about what Rob was saying? About your parents?" George asked softly.

"I really don't know," I said, feeling defeated. "I want to know, but I'm scared to find out."

"If you want, I can be there when you ask them," George offered.

I smiled. "Thank you. Maybe."

"How is it at home?" George asked.

"It's alright. I still haven't been able to talk to them about anything serious, though. Telling them about you was the most real thing I've said to them for ages," I said.

"I'm sorry," George said, reaching for my hand.

"It's not your fault."

"I don't care. I'm still sorry."

"Thanks. And anyway, I've got you."

"And I have you," he said, leaning his head on top of mine.

We both laughed together, and my heart swelled, enjoying the feeling of just being able to laugh, releasing everything except George, my hand in his, our laughs filling the space around us.

I pulled away and looked into George's eyes. I never really realised they were so blue. They were like the summer sky when no clouds were visible for miles. My eyes drifted to his lips, and I bit mine slightly.

"What's wrong?" George asked.

"Nothing. Absolutely nothing."

I leant in, slowly, carefully, and I saw him do the same. I closed my eyes and pressed my lips to his. They were warm and smooth and tasted like candy floss. I felt his lips tremble, or was it mine? I wasn't sure. I could tell he was nervous, but I was too, and I didn't mind. He kissed me back, his arms pulling me closer to him.

We broke for air, our lips still almost touching, but only to kiss again, still softly and tentatively but passionately all the same.

Slowly I pulled back, breathing quickly, my heartbeat a million times faster than it should be. George kissed me on the nose and wrapped me in his arms again as I leant against him.

I sighed slightly in amazement.

I'd just had my first kiss.

I closed my eyes for a moment, my head against his chest, savouring the feeling of pure joy and happiness and marvelling at what had just happened. My chest felt fluttery and light and the remaining worries I had seemed to evaporate away.

I opened my eyes again to see George looking down at me with a smile on his lips.

"What was that for?" he asked, still smiling.

"What, I need a reason to kiss you?" I said, laughing.

"Of course you don't."

"Good."

We lapsed into a comfortable silence, while all my nerves in my body were buzzing from the kiss.

18

A few minutes, or hours, later — time seemed to have lost all meaning — I saw a black, shiny car, tall and wide, out of the corner of my eye.

"That's my mum," I said, nodding in the direction of her car.

I felt like George and I were sitting too close. The gap between us was almost non-existent, but instead of shuffling away, I inched closer, closing the gap.

I no longer cared if she saw us together. She'd met George and she seemed to like him, and I hoped she understood how much he meant to me. I wasn't scared of her. But, I still felt like she could tell that just minutes ago, we'd kissed.

I pulled away from George, and his arm dropped from around me, but we still had our hands clasped together.

She parked the car just a few feet away from where George and I were sitting, and I squeezed his hand, then stood up, about to say goodbye to George before going over to slide in the car.

But the car door clicked and my mum pushed it open, swinging out her legs and standing up, before shutting the door behind her and walking over to us, a mischievous smile playing at her lips.

"Hello, George, Zoe," she said, the model of politeness.

"Hi," both George and I said.

I wasn't sure why she'd gotten out of the car, rather than just pick me up as normal, but I was sure there was a reason.

"Was I not supposed to come now?" My mum said, her eyebrows furrowed. "Were you two going to do something again?"

"Oh, no. We just…found each other, and George said he'd stay with me until you came," I said, deliberately leaving out what had happened with Rob.

"That's nice then," she said. But then she actually looked at me, clearly properly looked — probably to see if I was lying — and maybe she saw the tear stains on my cheeks or the clouded look in my eyes because she carried on. "Zoe, are you alright?"

I sucked in a breath, unsure what to say. George gave my hand a squeeze, and I looked over at him to see him smiling at me. "Um, well. I'm fine now. This boy in my year just pinned me to the wall and started saying some weird stuff, that's all." I didn't want to go into that all now. I wanted to tell both my parents together, knowing I'll be more likely to get an answer if they're both there.

"Oh dear. Who was it?" She asked.

"Someone called Robert Cooksley. Rob. I don't know him," I said.

My mum's eyes widened momentarily before she recovered herself, but she muttered something under her breath that I couldn't quite make out.

"What?" I asked.

"Nothing. Nothing," she said, shaking her head. But I knew there was more to it than that. There had to be. It was obvious she at least recognised the name, probably more than simply that, considering her reaction.

"Who is he?" I asked quizzically, suspicion weaved thickly into my voice.

"Please, can we talk about this with your father?" My mum asked, almost pleading.

I looked at her for a moment, reluctant to let her get away with it, but also knowing she wouldn't say anything until my dad was there. "Fine. Whatever," I said flatly.

"Thank you."

George cleared his throat awkwardly, clearly aware of the tension. My mum looked between us and then she smiled again, the tension gone from her face.

"Have you got any plans for tonight?" My mum asked George. I had a good idea where this was going, and I wasn't sure if I liked the thought or not.

"No, I don't think so," George replied, tentatively.

"Terrific," my mum said, smiling more brightly. "Would you like to come home with us for dinner? We can drop you home afterwards."

"Um. Sure. I'll have to check with my mum, though," George said after a beat.

My mum nodded as George reached into his blazer pocket and pulled out his phone, along with a few other bits that he quickly shoved deeply back into his pocket again — to be forgotten.

The glow illuminated his face in the growing darkness when George switched on his phone. I had been so busy concentrating on George and all that had happened that day, that I didn't even notice the sun sinking below the horizon, ready to close curtains, covered in stars, around the world.

His fingers danced around the screen, typing out a message to his parents. We were all quiet, and my mum softly tapped her foot against the floor. It was only a minute or so later that his phone pinged, and a smile lit up his face.

"I'd love to come; my mum says it's ok. As long as I'm home by ten," George said, smiling.

"Great," My mum said, looking quite excited.

"Thank you so much," George said kindly.

"Just get in the back of the car and we'll go."

George pulled the door open and slid in and I walked around to the other side of the car. I smiled at my mum before walking around, and she smiled back, and I couldn't help but feel surprised at how nice she was being.

I got in the car in the back next to George and pulled the door closed behind me. I put my hand on his lap; he placed his hand on top of mine and used his thumb to slowly trace circles around my hand, massaging it.

The front driver's door opened and my mum's head appeared in the gap.

"I'll just phone your dad and tell him the plan and then we can go," she said. I nodded, then she softly closed the door again and walked a few steps away from the car before making the phone call. I could see her lips moving but couldn't hear a word she said.

"Sorry in advance for anything that might happen," I said sheepishly, already worrying about what may unfold.

"Honestly, don't worry about it. You have enough things to worry about. Everything is going to be alright," George said, his voice as gentle as a feather falling from the sky.

"I hope so," I said, desperately hoping it would be alright.

"I know so," he said. "Come here."

He outstretched his arm so I shuffled along the seat and leant into his body and he wrapped his arm around me.

He ran his fingers through my hair, over and over, and the repetitive process helped calm my racing thoughts. He lowered his head slightly to press his lips against the top of my head, and that simple show of affection made my heart melt.

We didn't say anything else, just sat in the car waiting for my mum to finish. Though I couldn't hear her words, I could see the tension etched into her face and she seemed flustered. I figured she was telling my Dad about Rob, warning him maybe. But I tried not to think about that now. Not long after, the driver's door opened and my mum climbed into the seat. "All set," she said, overly enthusiastically.

I shuffled away from George to sit in my seat, and I reached around for the seatbelt, clicking it into place. As my mum pulled away, I tried to focus on George beside me and forget about Rob and what he had to do with me and my family. I reminded myself that George was with me, and with him there, everything would be alright.

19

We sat in the car in silence, only the sound of my too-fast beating heart and the roaring car engine filling my ears. Mine and George's hands' were clasped together, and he was using his thumb to draw circles on my hand, which had an unusual but welcome calming effect.

But I still couldn't quite calm down, Rob's words still echoing around my head and my mum's shocked face at the mention of his name. It was unnerving.

George clearly noticed how tense I was because he mouthed, "Are you ok?"

I nodded, trying to seem as relaxed as possible, knowing I wasn't doing a very good job at it. He looked back at me and raised his eyebrows in an "I-know-you're-lying" look. I sighed inwardly at how well he knew me.

I just smiled at him, knowing he could easily guess what was on my mind and I received a loving smile in return. My heart swelled at how understanding George was. I didn't need to explain myself for him to get me — he just did.

"So," I said, trying to sound as casual as possible. "How was your day?" I didn't want my mum commenting on our quiet, knowing that level of awkwardness wouldn't be ideal.

"It was ok, I guess. Boring lessons, though, as usual," George said. "How was yours?"

I raised my eyebrows at him. "That was a stupid question, I'm sorry. Of course, you had a rubbish day," George said, giving me a sympathetic look.

"Actually, it was a pretty good day until…" I trailed off. He knew exactly what I meant and I couldn't force my mouth to say anything about it.

"That's something. How was trampolining?" he said, kindly ignoring my inability to talk about what happened with Rob. I knew I'd have to later, with my parents, but that was later and I didn't need to think about that just yet.

"It was really fun, actually. Lauren started going through a new routine with me which has a lot of cool stuff in it and Zack was even nicer this time. We've fallen back into the rhythm of it now, so it's normal again," I said, smiling at the memory.

"That's good, I'm glad." He smiled kindly, and we carried on chatting more about it and his music and, before long, we arrived at my house.

My mum pulled into the drive and we all jumped out. I led the way, unhooking the latch on the wooden gate to find Pumpkin, my dog, barking like it was going to save the world, to welcome us. Her silky black fur shimmered under the light coming from the house and her long, thin tail wagged back and forth so fast it became a blur.

She ran up to me, tongue flailing, and jumped up on my knees, her front legs resting on my thighs. She was quite a lot too big to do this by now, but I didn't mind, I liked the comfort. I rested her legs back on the floor, though, before her rough paws could snag my trampolining leggings.

"Hey Pumpkin," I said, running my fingers through her fur.

The moment George saw Pumpkin, his eyes immediately lit up. He walked up to her, touched his fingertips to her fur and her head swung round to look at him, jumping up and down at the sight of George: love at first sight. Her tail moved even faster than before if that's even possible, and she licked George's hand enthusiastically.

"She's really sweet, can I keep her?" George said, laughing.

"No! She's mine," I laughed, walking over to join him and Pumpkin.

I took his hand in mine and gently pulled him away from her think, soft fur, leading him up the path curving to the front of my house and through the tall, wooden door, softly clicking it shut behind us.

•••

I was sitting on the faded brown leather sofa in our living room, with George next to me and my parents sitting on the sofa opposite. My dad was polite when we first came into the house, introducing himself to George and asking some questions to get to know him a little when we moved into the lounge. I didn't say much, but rather sat listening and trying to quell the anxiety for the oncoming conversation.

I knew I had to bring up the inevitable conversation about Rob, and I'd either find out what they'd been hiding from me, or they'd lie and then I'd wonder what it was. I didn't know which would be worse.

But that wasn't the only thing I wanted to talk to my parents about. I knew that telling them about how much I was struggling was long overdue. They needed to know how it was for me, and that included telling them their part in it. It needed to be done.

When there was a lull in the conversation, I suddenly took a breath, knowing I needed to do this for myself. It would be better with George by my side, anyway, I thought. Now was as good a time as any.

"Can I just say something, please?" I said, almost pleading. I knew it was a risk and there was a chance I'd crumple into a million pieces while I was talking, but it was a risk I was willing to take.

My parents looked at each other, slightly confused at the serious tone of my voice. My mum hesitated before looking at me, saying, "Okay, then."

I looked at each of my parents, in turn, holding their eyes for a few moments so they'd know I was serious. I took another deep breath, trying to fill my lungs with as much air as possible, knowing that a couple of minutes later I wouldn't be able to breathe at all. I looked over at George, and when our eyes locked, I tried to use some of his strength and comfort to urge me onwards. He smiled at me, and I nodded before turning back to my parents.

"Ok, so. I'm really struggling. With everything," I paused. Took another deep breath. "I feel as though I'm barely staying afloat. It's a little better now, having George and Emily are helping, but I'm still not ok. And, I'm sorry, but you two don't help. You're always putting so much pressure on me and I feel I can't talk to you about anything because you never seem to care about how I'm doing. Have you even noticed how I never tell you anything? Or how I've only started doing things again in the last few weeks, but not the past few years? Did you even wonder why, or bother to ask me about it? You never asked why I stopped talking about Jane, and you should have. You shouldn't have made me feel so alone."

I felt tears prick in the back of my eyes but I fought them, refusing to break down in front of my parents. Nobody said anything. A stunned silence settled around us and I felt the walls starting to close in, suffocating. I didn't know how much longer I'd be able to hold it back, and after another moment passed, the worry and panic crashed down on me, a deathly weight.

I stood and walked out, forcing my legs to keep walking, despite their protests, up the stairs and the few more meters to my room. When I crossed the threshold, I stopped. I couldn't breathe. My throat was tight, blocked, and I couldn't do anything about it. I rocked back and forth on my heels like somehow that would bring my breath back. I attempted to take deep breaths, but my lungs felt shrivelled, not co-operating. Just as I thought I would pass out, footsteps quietly echoed from the stairs. I wondered, with irrational hope, whether it was my mum, coming back to cheer up her precious daughter. But, no. Of course it wasn't.

Just as George appeared in the doorway I collapsed on my bed, realising tears were streaming down my face. I somehow remembered how to breathe again, but my heart thumped so loudly in my chest, I worried that it would explode. I turned away from him, facing the wall, even though I knew he didn't mind. The bed sunk

118

slightly with his added weight, the mattress shifting beneath me, and the next thing I knew, his arms were around me, his soft gentle hands stroking my hair. We were both facing the wall, and I curled into his body behind me, grateful for the comfort it provided. The tears were still falling rapidly, landing on the pillow.

After a few more minutes, I slowly turned over and he lifted his arms to allow me to wriggle around. I faced him, but I didn't look at his face. I couldn't bring myself to look into his endless blue eyes. Instead, I focussed on his tie: how it was loosened slightly, more than the usual school standards, probably done by his careful fingers before band practice. Then those same fingers played the guitar, beautiful sounds leaping into the air, dancing. I stared at the navy blue material, the same colour as the PE top I was wearing from trampolining, and I reminded myself of that feeling of weightlessness, when flying, and anything else, seemed entirely possible, and everything was filled with this hopeful possibility.

Eventually, the tears stopped falling. But I didn't stop looking at George's tie, at the material knotted around itself that I knew he did over and over sometimes to get it just right.

He lightly wiped his thumb under my eyes to dry off the tears, his touch soft. I finally looked up at him, labouringly bringing my eyes up to meet his. But when he smiled at the simple movement, it was worth the effort.

"They seem genuinely worried about you, you know. When you left, your mum started to cry. I went after you then but, honestly, they seem quite sorry." George had his hand resting on my arm, and he started rubbing my arm gently, up and down, up and down, and his rough fingers reminded me that he was here, with me, and I could count on him.

I didn't say anything, though. I couldn't seem to move my mouth to form any words.

"Why did you decide to tell them after all this time?" He spoke gently, calmly, like he knew how close I was to shattering again.

I looked at him for a moment before I spoke, trying to gather my racing thoughts into comprehensible words.

"I guess I've wanted to say something for ages, but I haven't known how. I knew they should know, and they should know the impact they have, too. I also wouldn't have been able to do it on my own. I needed you there to help me." Only after I said it, did I realise how true it was. I leant closer to George, even though we were already touching, and hid my face in his shirt, wishing I could stay there forever, but knowing I couldn't.

"You are so brave. The way you stood up to them like that, that took huge amounts of courage. You know that, right?" I nodded slightly, only half meaning it. I didn't feel brave.

"Before I left, they said they'd call us when dinner was ready and we can talk then." I just nodded again. I didn't want to eat anything, even though my stomach was growling and the emptiness threatened to consume me. But most of all, I didn't want to talk to them and face the aftermath of what I'd said. Telling them was one thing, but explaining myself was another entirely.

All of a sudden, I felt so guilty about dragging George into this mess. It wasn't his choice.

"I'm sorry you have to deal with all this. With me and all my mess. I shouldn't be putting so much pressure on you to make me alright, I'm sorry. Maybe I'm meant to be broken," I said, almost a whisper, scared at the weight of the words that were falling out my mouth. I'd thought them so many times, but I never thought I'd actually tell him I felt like that. "I'm sorry," I said again.

"Don't apologise. Please, never apologise for your feelings, or being yourself, ok?" His voice was firm, pleading. I nodded numbly, not sure I'd really taken in the full effect of his words. "I'm not leaving you. I'm not scared of a little messiness. But you're not supposed to be broken, I promise."

Somehow, in that moment, I couldn't wrap my head around the fact that he didn't care about any of that, and he wasn't going to leave me because of it. It felt like a foreign concept. "But you shouldn't have to deal with this."

"Neither should you."

And I swear my heart melted.

20

We were both leaning against my bed, sitting on the soft carpeted floor of my room, and I rested my head on George's shoulder, taking his hand in mine.

I tried to see my room from George's perspective, seeing my lilac walls and the photographs pegged to ribbon, the fluffy fairy lights from when I was younger but didn't have the heart to get rid of. The bookcase was full of books — my favourites and ones I was yet to read — with ornaments and candles in front of the titles, the photo frames with quotes from those books inside instead of photos, my drawings pinned to the pin-board at the end of my bed. I liked my room, it was very me, and I hoped George thought so too.

With him in my room, it triggered a memory.

"Can I ask you something?" I said warily.

"Of course. What is it?" George said, his voice gentle, kind.

"Remember that night when I told you I liked you?" I said slowly. I had been sitting on the floor, leaning against the bed, that night, similar to where we were sitting. The unlikeliness of the situation didn't escape me.

"How could I forget?"

"Well... Was I just a crush to you then?" I said, wishing I'd kept quiet, scared of the answer.

"Why would you ask that?" He asked teasingly. I answered him anyway.

"Because I've never been the best person or the person who people go to and because people always leave me for someone better and I'm never the first choice," I said, almost in a whisper, well aware of the rambling note to my voice.

"Zoe, when I first saw you, properly, I thought that you were the most beautiful girl I'd ever seen. So, yes, I guess it was just a crush at first. But that was in year 10, in that first English lesson. I remember how you kept your head down, never saying a word accept to answer the register, but you scribbled down notes and answers with such a ferocious passion that I was jealous of your obvious spark. I was so intrigued by you. All I wanted to do was get to know you better." His voice sounded wistful at the memory, soft and nostalgic and I couldn't help but smile a little, even though I struggled to fully believe his words. I lifted my head off his shoulder and shuffled to face him. He was smiling, seemingly subconsciously.

"It took me a few lessons to steel my nerves enough to talk to you. And when I did, I could tell you were struggling with something so big that it hunched your shoulders and quietened your voice. And I wanted to help, I wanted so badly to make you believe in yourself, but I didn't know how. But I kept on trying and I loved getting to know you more and more. And my feelings for you quickly developed into more than just a silly crush."

He squeezed my hand, emphasising his words. But I couldn't look at him. I thought about how I was last year, barely talking or letting anyone know anything. I felt so guilty for making George work so hard to find out even small things about me, how persistent he must have been to break down the walls I'd built around myself. And I didn't even notice.

"Why didn't you give up?" I asked. I gave up on myself in less time than that, and he carried on trying. I couldn't even grasp it.

"Because you're worth the effort. Zoe, you're so amazing. You were amazing even before you gained some confidence, and you're amazing now. I can't even imagine not wanting to be with you."

I could tell he was looking at my face, but I was looking at our hands, clasped together. I was at a loss for words.

He lifted his other hand to my chin, putting his fingers below it and lifting my face up so that I was looking at him. But I still positioned my eyes to look at his shirt, not meeting his eyes.

"Look at me," he said gently. I resisted for a beat, but then I pulled my eyes up to meet his, and the blue depths greeted me warmly.

"What did I ever do to deserve you?" I said, my voice soft and quiet.

"You were you. That's all."

I smiled.

"Now, listen to me. I wouldn't change you for the world, ok? You're perfect just the way you are. And I promise I mean that. Will you ever believe me?" His voice was stern and gentle at the same time and I wanted so badly to believe him. But I didn't know if I could.

"Honestly, probably not. But there's a chance. Maybe," I said softly. Guilt flooded through me again. I knew it would be simpler if I just believed him, for both of us, but I didn't want to lie either.

He made a strange face, almost like a grimace, and then sighed. "That's what I thought."

I didn't say anything.

Muffled voices came up from the living room, and I wondered what my parents were saying downstairs, but I figured I wouldn't want to know anyway, so I quickly stopped that thought process. Would they ever forgive me? Would they ever look at me the same again? Would they think I need to be treated differently? I couldn't stop the damning questions in my head.

"Will I be alright?" I whispered, barely audible.

"Of course you'll be alright. You're alright now," George said sweetly and calmly.

"But I'm not. Nothing is alright at the moment."

"Come here," he said, outstretching his arms. I turned to face away from him and then leant into his body, resting my head on his chest and gladly letting his arms wrap around me. He ran his fingers through my hair a few times and I put my hands on top of his when they rested on my shoulder. He took my mind off my parents, even if only for a minute.

"Honey, they won't hate you. No one will hate you. No one could ever hate you," he whispered delicately.

"But what if they do?" I whispered, my voice sounding more worried than I would have liked.

"But they won't, trust me."

"You can't know that."

"No. So I'll just make sure they don't."

I turned my face so my cheek was resting on his chest and leant in closer to him. He held me tighter; like if he didn't I might have fallen apart in his arms.

His chest was so warm and I tried to fight the tears again. I wasn't sure of the exact reason for them this time but the barrier had been removed, and I'd have to face the river. He noticed the silent tears streaming down my face and used his warm thumb to wipe them away. It was a lost cause, though, because more tears replaced the ones he moved.

"What's wrong?" He asked sweetly.

"What's right?"

The corners of his lips went up in a small smile and I wanted to smile back, but I couldn't force my lips to move upwards. I felt so exhausted.

Tears rolled down my face in intervals that I couldn't control, despite how hard I tried.

"I think something's wrong with me. I can't stop crying," I whispered. After a moment, I added, solemnly, "I'm weak."

"Nothing's wrong with you. And you're not weak. You've just been strong for too long," he said gently, but with a firm tone, that made the seriousness clear.

"Isn't that a quote or something?" I said, vaguely attempting to lighten the atmosphere a little.

"Well, yeah. I may have looked at inspirational quotes to use to try and make you feel better," he said embarrassed and guiltily. I imagined the blush rising in his cheeks behind me.

"Thank you. That's very sweet," I simply said, smiling. I wanted to say so much more, but I didn't know how to express the warmth flowing through me at the thought of what he'd done for me.

126

The tears slowly started to subside as George lightly traced random patterns across my hands and wrists. For a minute I wondered what I looked like: probably an absolute mess with my makeup run down my face and my hair a big mass of knots. I wondered if George would think I was pretty then.

I grudgingly moved away from George and, without standing up, reached for my hairbrush. "Wouldn't want them thinking I've been crying, would I?" I said sarcastically. But it was true. I never cried in front of my parents. Not anymore.

I ran the brush through my thick, knotted hair a few times, but I wasn't getting anywhere. I felt my composure start to crumble and fall at my apparent inability to do something as simple as brush my hair. But before I could get angry or upset and start ripping my hair out, George reached his hand out to my hand that was wrapped around the brush and gently tugged at it. I slowly let go and he took my hand to shuffle me closer to him again. He turned me around so I was facing away from him and then he started to brush my hair. Lightly and slowly; over and over. It was oddly soothing and managed to calm me. Only then did I realise that I'd been shaking ever so slightly. My body stilled like George was casting a spell over me to silence my worries.

"I'm glad I don't have long hair like this. It's so much effort!" George said, laughing, after a minute or two of brushing my hair therapeutically.

"I know. It's a nightmare sometimes." But I was laughing too.

He continued to brush my hair and after another minute, the brush stopped getting caught on the knots.

He handed the brush back to me, saying, "All done, honey."

"That's twice today," I said, turning around to face him.

"What is?" He asked, confused.

"That's the second time you called me 'honey'."

"Don't you like it?" He asked, suddenly sounding anxious and embarrassed.

"No, no. I love it. It's really sweet." I said quickly. He relaxed again, just as suddenly as he'd become tense.

"Good. And I just thought it might be cute," he said. He reached his hand out and tucked my hair behind my ear, then rested his hand there, cupping my face in his hand.

"Thank you," I said softly. "But I need to wash my face."

"Ok," he said, smiling and lightly brushing my cheek with his thumb. But I didn't move.

The desperate urge to kiss him washed over me; an electrical current pulsing through my veins.

I stretched my neck up so our faces were only an inch apart and he lowered his head slightly, too; leaning in. Before I knew it, he pressed his soft lips to mine. Even though this was the second time we'd kissed that day, the pressure consumed me entirely; enveloping me in the brilliance of the moment. We broke away but only moved about a centimetre. Our noses brushed each other's and our lips were almost touching. I smiled and I could feel his lips move upwards, too.

He still had my face in his hands, and I leant into his touch gratefully.

"They'll call us soon," I said. "I'll be right back."

128

I reluctantly stood up and walked to the bathroom, shutting the door behind me. I looked at myself in the mirror for a few moments, staring at the makeup streaks running down my face. I quickly looked away.

I scrubbed off all my makeup, pressing too hard and too fast until all the traces vanished. I didn't care that it made my face even more red and blotchy than it already was from the crying, I just wanted it gone. Like I could rub away all that had happened with Rob, leaving only the pureness that George provided.

I splashed water on my face in a vague hope to even it out, but I didn't put any more makeup on.

I looked at myself again, forcing my eyes to stay focused and not drift away. I took a deep breath, seeing myself suck in the air through my nose and release it out my mouth. Again and again, in, out, nose, mouth. I leant my back against the wall behind me, and slid down to the floor, folding my legs in front of me. I needed a minute before I went back out there. I shut my eyes, putting my forehead on my knees and tapping my fingers anxiously on my other arm.

I sat there for a minute or two, then, with a shaky intake of breath, pushed myself up and gripped the sink in front of me, willing myself to not flip out. I took a deep breath, in a last-ditch effort to calm all my nerves, and slowly walked back to my bedroom to join George.

"You really don't need makeup, love. You're beautiful as it is," George said as I walked into the room. I smiled a little and sat next to him, leaning my head on his shoulder again, his warm arms loosely wrapped around me.

He lightly pressed his lips to the top of my head, so soft and gentle I could barely feel it. The sides of my lips automatically rose at his touch, and I wondered, fleetingly, if he had any idea of the effect he had on me.

I lifted my head to face him and looked into his eyes. The brilliant blue shocked me, once again, and I couldn't help but internally gawk at his perfect beauty.

We kissed again, and I pulled him close to me, my hands on his back and his on mine. I felt oddly at ease, considering all I had waiting for me downstairs, but those things didn't matter when I had my lips pressed against George's. We broke apart before things could get any further, and I smiled at him warmly.

"You're perfect," I breathed, so quietly I could barely hear the words.

"Not as perfect as you," he sighed, just as quietly. I smiled, not even thinking about the fact that the words were lies.

I lowered my head again, resting it on his shoulder. He tucked a few stray strands of my hair behind my ear, clearing my cheek and lightly circled it with his thumb.

"Zoe," my mum shouted up the stairs, startling me and making George jump slightly.

"Coming," I shouted back, hoping she couldn't hear the breathlessness in my voice.

"Ready to face the trial?" he asked, pushing himself off the floor. I didn't move.

I sighed. "Might as well just get it over with, I guess. I can't avoid this forever," I said. George took my hand and pulled me up, and I stumbled a little.

"You'll be ok," he said, squeezing my hand and peering into my eyes.

I nodded stiffly, trying desperately to keep it together. Breathe, I told myself. Beneath my body, my knees chattered, like when the piercing cold wraps its icy fingers around them. The anxiety inside of me fought to take control, but George's hand managed to keep the panic attack from overruling me. My stomach twisted uncomfortably and it took a lot of effort to keep nausea from taking over. My eyes stared into George's, trying to find his hope and sanity to help me find mine. I saw it in his eyes then. They sparkled and shone, showing that he believed it would be alright. All I needed to do was grasp that hope for myself; then I'd be ok.

Quickly, I took a step forward and threw my arms around his neck, holding him against my body so tightly it surely must have hurt him. But he didn't complain and I needed the contact too much. He wrapped his arms around me, too, and rested his hands on the back of my head, taking some of my hair in his fists. For what felt like the hundredth time that day, I wanted to freeze the moment and stay in it forever. But I pulled away reluctantly and settled on holding his hand, curling my hands around his wrists instead.

With a horrible dread heavy in my chest and my arms wrapped around George's to keep my sanity, we walked down the stairs slowly, trying to delay the inevitable for as long as our luck would allow.

21

We sat at the kitchen table, no one daring to be the first to talk about the inevitable. We chatted about other, inconsequential things, but not the things which really mattered. But I was starting to get twitchy, my anxiety threatening to take over, and all I wanted to do was get it over with. It wasn't worth delaying anymore; I was just making it worse for myself, and probably everyone else. But just as I was about to say something, my mum talked first. "If we're all finished, then shall we go and sit in the other room?" She said, a thousand times too cheery. We all nodded silently in agreement.

I started to pick up my plate and reach over for George's, but my mum interrupted me, saying, "Oh, don't worry about that! We'll sort it out later."

I gently placed the plates back on the table, restraining myself from furrowing my eyebrows at the request. My mum always wanted the table cleared as soon as we were all finished, and the difference stumped me.

I stood up, and George took that as a cue for him to do the same. Tapping his hand to get his attention, I nodded my head to the living room and we walked the few steps it took to get there. I slumped on the sofa, crossing my legs in a tight pretzel-like position under my body. George sat down, too, loosely folding his legs beside him. I resisted the urge to hold his hand, unsure of how to act in front of my parents. It all felt even more forced and unnatural than it did earlier that day.

My parents were whispering in the next room, but I couldn't make out any of the words; nothing but inaudible mumbles.

"It'll be alright," George whispered, softly rubbing my knee with his hand.

"I'm not so sure," I whispered back. My breathing was gradually quickening and I didn't know if I could keep the panic under control much longer. My hands started to shake, and my chest tightened and suddenly the fear of a panic attack washed over me and for a moment I didn't know what to do. I could feel George's hand on my knee, but it did little to comfort me.

"Breathe," he said gently. I focused all my attention on my breathing, trying to count the seconds I held each breath for. I instantly felt the benefit of it. After only a few deep breaths, my chest loosened and the shakes started to subside. I thought about this caring and beautiful boy beside me, helping me feel better about myself, helping me through the panic, and keeping me sane. He was my gravity, the one keeping me the right way up, the one keeping me from drowning.

"Thank you," I said to him, after fully regaining my control. "Thank you for everything."

He smiled at me, causing my heart to flutter like a butterfly in the wind.

He held my hand with one of his and he ran his fingers along my veins with the other. It calmed me further, and I didn't feel so overwhelmed by the situation.

"You'll be ok. I'm here," George whispered. But before I could say anything, my parents walked into the room.

They sat down opposite us as they did earlier, and I concentrated on my breathing; trying to keep my anxiety under the surface. My parents didn't say anything for a moment, but rather awkwardly looked between each other.

George started to take his hand away from mine, but I couldn't bear that, so I squeezed, holding on tighter, curling my fingers around his own, emphasising the fact that I needed his comfort. I didn't care if it wasn't proper, or the right thing to do in the situation. All I cared about was that I wasn't alone.

My mum broke the silence first. "We need to talk about this. But first, we need to apologise," she said gently, but with a harsh tone weaved in as well. When I didn't say anything, she continued. "I realise now how oblivious we've been. We weren't there for you when you needed us, and I wish it weren't that way. But that's the past, and I want to make the future different. I feel like I've lost you—" yeah, and who's fault is that? I thought despite myself, "—and I want you back, darling. But I can only do that if you let me." It sounded like she might cry, and for a moment, pain flashed in her eyes, but she took another breath and it was gone before I could even be sure it was there in the first place.

I thought about what she'd said for a moment, and my heart fluttered at the idea of really having my mum back, in a way I should have always had her. But the past couldn't be changed.

134

"I'd like that," I said at last, and she let out a breath I didn't realise she'd been holding. "But, I'd like some answers first," I added firmly, thinking of Rob. This seemed like a good time.

"Of course, darling. Ask whatever you like," she said. But there was a clear note of anxiety in her voice, and I tried to pretend it wasn't there.

I took a deep breath, knowing this could be something that might have jump-started my anxiety again.

"Who's Robert Cooksley?" I asked.

My dad visibly paled at the name, and my mum winced again, though they must have known what was coming.

"Why do you ask?" My dad said, his voice tight and strained.

"This boy in my year cornered me after trampolining today and said how he should have been the one with the good family and how I ignored him. I'd never seen him before, and when he realised I didn't know him, he kept on saying sorry, and how it wasn't his place to tell me. He said to ask my parents. So, I'm asking you. Who's Robert Cooksley?" I felt oddly empowered, because, although I knew I wouldn't like what I was going to hear, I was glad I wasn't the only one who was uncomfortable. My dad squirmed, seeming to shrink away from the name.

However, when my dad struggled to form any words, the anxiety suddenly felt overwhelming, and I had to use a great deal of strength to push it back down again.

"Listen, Zoe. I'm sorry, but there's something that we haven't told you. Something that maybe we should have," my dad said carefully.

When he didn't go on, I prompted, "What is it?"

He seemed to take a moment to gather himself, form the correct words in his head, before speaking. "Robert is… he's my son."

My jaw dropped.

"Wh— What?" I stammered, but couldn't muster anything more substantial than that. I felt my world crumbling down, like everything I knew was suddenly burning and crashing around me and there wasn't a single thing I could do to stop it.

"He's about seven months younger than you," my dad said like somehow this was an explanation.

"How?" I was so, so confused.

"I'm sorry to admit, but I made a mistake. A really, really big mistake. Your mum was pregnant with you and we got into a pretty bad fight. I left the house to get away, but I got really drunk — I'm not saying that as an excuse, I'm really not. I got talking to this woman, and one thing led to another..." he trailed off, as we all filled in the blank.

"Anyway," he continued. "Your mum and I made up, but I didn't say anything about that night. I could barely remember it, and I didn't want to ruin anything more than I already had. But then the woman from the pub, her name was Marian, got in contact and told me she was pregnant. I couldn't believe it. But when I told her I was already married, with a child and another on the way, she flipped out. She said she didn't want me to have anything to do with her or the baby."

He took a breath, and I could see how this story was affecting him. But I needed to know, even though my heart rate was speeding up and my palms started to feel sweaty.

"I felt I had to tell your mum what had happened, and we worked through that eventually. Marian called me when the baby was born, just to say that he was healthy, his name and that they were both moving to Australia to be closer to her parents. That's the last I heard from either of them. I assumed they'd still be there, but… well, clearly they're back."

I leant forward in my chair, resting my elbows on my knees and my chin on my hands. "So he's my half-brother?" I asked eventually, dumbfounded, wishing it weren't true.

"Yes, he is," my dad confirmed.

I felt betrayed, lost. I realised afterwards that it must have been something like that, from piecing together what Rob had said to me, but hearing it be confirmed, from my dad, was a whole other situation. It all made sense, why Rob was so angry at me, jealous of me. My dad should have been a part of his life, too. But he'd had his father ripped away from him. And he thought I knew who he was but had failed to talk to him. Of course, he was angry at me, I should have acknowledged him, had I known who he was. And it explained why he ran away when he realised what he'd done, what he'd revealed to me.

And suddenly that anger that Rob had felt towards me, I felt it towards my parents, a harsh fire raging within me. "Why didn't you tell me?" I asked, my voice a dangerous quiet.

"We didn't want to hurt you, sweetie," my mum said, trying to stay calm.

"Were you ever going to tell me?" I demanded. I distantly felt George's hand in my back, reassuring me of his presence and his comfort. I'd almost forgotten he was there.

"I don't know," my dad said after a moment.

"Does Grace know?" I asked at last. The anger had already rippled away a little, but the confusion and hurt were still heavy inside me.

"Yes, she does. We made her promise not to tell you," my dad said. He sounded like he regretted it.

But that didn't make it better.

They'd lied to me.

Something else hit me. So hard it knocked the breath out of me and I felt like I was falling.

"How could you?" I said to my dad. My voice felt hollow and weak. "How could you cheat on mum?"

But I couldn't wait for an answer. I couldn't stay under control anymore. I'd held it off for too long already. My palms suddenly felt clammy and my vision narrowed slightly. It was happening again. But this time some deep breaths wouldn't have stopped it.

In the far away distance, I heard my mother's worried voice saying, "Is she okay? What's happening?"

And George's voice, closer, but still distant, replied, "She's having a panic attack."

Now they know, I thought. It only made my breathing shallower and my insides tighter. I could still hear voices, but they were muffled and I couldn't make out any words.

I stood up in a daze and walked out, for the second time that day, and clumsily stumbled to the front door. I

138

pulled on the handle, fumbling, and stepped outside. There was a bench a few feet away from the door, so I made my way there unsteadily and slumped into it. I tried, desperately, to suck air into my lungs, and I was vaguely aware of my ragged breathing, but I didn't know what to do to stop it.

I have a brother, the thought replayed over in my head, much like Rob's damning instructions to talk to my parents. I rocked back and forth, my hands pressed to my face, desperately trying to get through this as best I could.

Somehow, through the circling thoughts and the raging panic, I felt oddly comforted. I had a brother, and this time the thought didn't scare me. I'd met him, and though our first meeting wasn't exactly ideal, I felt a blossom of excitement at the idea of getting to know a brother I didn't know I had.

I looked up, seeing through my fingers, and focused on the sky. It was a deep shade of blue, teetering on the verge of black, tiny stars sparkling on the dark canvas; the moon was a perfect crescent, a bright yellow-white shine.

I didn't hear his footsteps, only when he sat down next to me did I realise I had company. I peeked at George through the gaps in my fingers, and I took my hands away from my face, instead leaning against the back of the bench. After another moment, I put my hand on his lap, and he entwined his fingers in mine, and that extra bit of comfort made breathing easier again.

It took me a few more minutes to calm down fully. "Sorry," I said after my breathing had returned to somewhere close to normal.

"What are you sorry for, exactly?" He asked carefully.

"Everything."

"That's too vague," he said teasingly.

"I'm sorry for making a scene and freaking out, and that you keep on having to come and help me out of my panic," I whispered, barely audible.

"Zoe," he started, shuffling closer to me, "we've been through this already, remember?"

I nodded. But guilt still gripped around my heart, heavy, bringing it down.

We sat there for a moment, listening to the ruffle of leaves, the tooting of owls, and the whistling wind.

"Do you think you're ready to go back in?" George asked.

"Yeah, I guess so," I grudgingly said.

He stood up, so gracefully it shocked me for a moment, and pulled me up to my feet after him. He laid one of his hands on the small of my back, supporting me.

Before we stepped through the door, and I was certain my parents couldn't see us, I stopped and reached for George's face, cupping it in my hands. Rising to my toes, I pressed my quivering lips to his.

•••

We walked into the living room to my parent's concerned faces gaping at me. I tried my best to ignore them, but it proved more difficult than I would have liked. I gave them what I hoped was a reassuring smile and received smiles back, so it must have had roughly the right effect.

I tried not to think of what my dad did.

"Are you okay, darling?" My mum asked, suddenly sounding much more motherly.

"Yeah," I whispered, but she didn't look convinced — I wouldn't be either.

"Was it finding out about Rob that caused it?" My dad asked guiltily.

I shrugged, but George answered for me. "She's been teetering on the edge of having an attack all afternoon, with a few small ones, too. It was almost inevitable that it would happen, it was just that that knocked her over the edge." I gave him an appreciative smile, glad of the small weight lifted off my shoulders.

"Why didn't you tell us these sort of things have been happening?" My mum asked, accusation badly hidden from her voice.

I shrugged, not even knowing the answer myself.

"How long has it been going on?" My dad asked nervously.

It took a second or two for me to think of the right answer and go through the maths, but eventually, I whispered, "About a year of these panic attacks. A few years of everything else."

No one said anything as my parents pondered how oblivious they'd been.

"I'm sorry," my mother finally said.

"That doesn't even cut it," I said bluntly, my voice growing stronger. I didn't care that I was being rude.

"You're right. So what will?" My mum questioned.

I thought about it but came up empty. What would cut it? I shrugged, deciding it was best to say nothing.

"Okay, so tell us when you've decided. But, for now, how about you tell us what's been going on? We want to help, I promise," My mum said.

So, I told them. Not everything, not even close. But some of the main things, like what had happened with Jane and how I was scared to get close to anyone before Emily and George. I told them a little about the bullying and how lonely I was and how much pressure I felt I was under.

I lost track of time, it didn't seem relevant as I was opening my heart for them to see, so I had no idea how long I spoke for. But once I finally felt I'd told them all I wanted to, my throat feeling tired and raw from the constant talking and feeling exhausted, my mum did something I thought she'd forgotten how to do. She walked up to me, sat beside me and threw her arms around me, causing warmth to flood through my veins.

22

I shrugged into my coat, ready to step into the bitterly cold night to take George home. I felt almost disorientated. I'd learnt so much that night and so much had changed. It was dizzying.

"Are you ok?" George asked, concern laced into his voice.

I nodded. Then changed my mind, saying, "I'm not sure. It's just a lot to process." That was an understatement.

George stepped towards me, closing the space between us and he lightly wrapped his arms around me. Leaning my head against his chest, I closed my eyes and savoured the moment, appreciating how perfectly my head fitted in the hollow of his neck and how natural it felt to be enclosed in his arms. I heard a faint cough, a clearing of someone's throat, and opened my eyes, turning my head to look behind me. I instantly blushed more than I would have thought possible, quickly letting go of George's soft, safe and caring embrace.

My mum stood behind us, a sweet smile on her face. "Come on, you two. We don't want George to be late, do we?" My mum said, trying to tease but making a poor attempt at it.

I smiled sheepishly at her, not sure what to do in this type of situation. I ran my hand down George's arm, stopping at his hand to hold it in my own. I led him to the front door, remembering the situation I was in the last time I walked through it. I took a deep breath, filling my lungs with the cool evening air, and pushed the memories away to the back of my mind, closing the door on them and locking them away with a key.

My mum chattered constantly in the front of the car while I rolled my eyes at every other comment she made. I didn't know what she was trying to achieve, but it seemed as though she was desperate to avoid any awkward silences this time.

George called out the directions at the appropriate moments, but my mum was never any good at navigation, so she went the wrong way a few times, despite George's clear instructions.

When we finally reached his house, I gasped.

Before me stood a Victorian cottage with glamorous arrays of flowers all over the garden. Long, lush ivy reached for the roof and hugged the walls, creating a cosy effect on the house. The windows had multiple squares of glass, separated by lines of white wood. Right in the middle was a small door, not much taller than George, and a small post-box sat on the wall, seemingly suspended in mid-air.

I thought my house was beautiful, but this cottage made my own look like a slum house compared to this palace.

"You like it?" George asked, seeing my awe. I just nodded vigorously, not sure what to say.

"I'm sure my parents would love to meet you," he said hopefully.

I hated to let him down, but I knew that if anything more happened that day, I'd struggle to cope with it. I didn't want the first time I met his parents to be a disaster because I became too overwhelmed. "I'm sorry, but not today. It's been a long day, and I don't know if I can manage anything else," I said, squeezing his hand.

"Of course, don't worry about it. We'll arrange another day, ok?" He said. I knew he'd understand, but I couldn't help but notice a slight hint of disappointment in his voice.

"Definitely, I promise," I said, looking into his eyes, though I could barely see them in the shadow created by the streetlight. "Thank you, for today."

He smiled at me and with a surge of courage, I leant between the seats and quickly kissed him. He seemed pleasantly surprised, and his smile widened.

"Thank you for the lift, Molly," George said kindly to my mum.

"You're welcome, George. It was lovely to meet you properly this time," she said, all politeness.

"You too," he said. He turned to me. "Bye, then. Let me know when you're home, ok?"

"Of course. Goodnight," I said. My heart swelled at the thought that he worried about me getting home safely, and it was a strange but not unpleasant feeling, being cared for so deeply.

"Goodnight." He pulled on the door handle and stepped out, and I watched him walk up the path, unlock the door and step in, but not before turning to me and waving. I waved back, not caring that he probably couldn't see me.

I slipped out of the back seat, pulling open the passenger door and sliding in there instead, fumbling with my seatbelt as my mum drove off, away from George's house.

"I like him. He really does seem to care about you," she said after we'd pulled out of his road.

"I'm glad," I said. And I really was. I wanted my parents to like George, and to understand how amazing he'd been to me, how much of a difference he'd made in my life.

After a beat, I said, "Listen, I'm really sorry for everything. I should have told you about what was going on with me, but I didn't know how. I didn't think you really cared, either." Sitting in that car, thinking about everything that I'd done wrong, guilt clawed at my stomach, slowly ripping it apart piece by piece.

"Zoe, of course we care. We care so, so much about you and what's going on in your life. You shouldn't be the one apologising. Your offence is far less bad, compared to what your father and I have done to you," she said, and the remorse and regret were clear in her voice. The anger flared again, but I swallowed it down.

"You know, your dad and I used to be friends with George's parents," my mum said.

My mouth dropped open, for at least the hundredth time that day. "What?"

"I know, I know. We met them before you were born, and then when you and George were born, you used to play together. We were quite close, seeing each other often, and you and George seemed to have so much fun."

I looked at her out of the corner of my eye, and she smiled, thinking of better times. "Wow," I said, unable

146

to come up with anything else. At least now, the fact she seemed so shocked to see George's mum that day in the park made sense.

"Wow indeed," my mum chuckled. "But then they found out about Rob—" she winced "—and we drifted apart. They couldn't understand why I stayed with your dad after what he did. They were both so angry at him, and it was always so tense when we met up. We lost contact eventually," she drifted off.

I took a deep breath, debating whether or not to ask the thing that I'd been desperate to. "Why did you stay with him?" I asked quietly.

She didn't say anything for a moment. Then she smiled. "Because I love him," she finally said.

And I couldn't say anything to that.

Because isn't love supposed to be what trumps all?

"It was hard, though. It took a while for me to trust him again, but I know your father. And I know he isn't the type of person who cheats on his wife or who wants to hurt his children. And, eventually, that was enough for me," my mum said, a slightly sad tone to her voice.

"He hasn't...?" I trailed off, unwilling to actually utter the words.

"Oh no, no, no. Definitely not. I trust him when he says it was only that once." The determined and convinced expression on her face further reassured me that my dad wasn't an awful person — just someone who made an awful mistake once. Not to say that Rob, as a person, was a mistake, but my dad cheating certainly was.

"Ok," I said, accepting her reasons for how she acted. I wasn't letting my dad get away with it quite so easily, though. I was still angry at him for what he put my mum through and how close he was to destroying our family.

"I want to help you. Help with your anxiety and any other problem you might have," she said after a while of silence. "I know we don't know each other that well at the moment, but I'd like to change that." I nodded and smiled, but I didn't say anything. I didn't know how she could help me now. It would take a while for her to get to know me again. But I thought I was willing to try.

We lapsed into silence and I tried to think of nothing at all.

23

We didn't get home until quite late, so I went straight to bed. I bade goodnight to my parents and then hurried upstairs before they could say anything more. I texted George to say I was home and I was going to sleep and thanked him for the day. I didn't wait for a reply. I got ready for bed in a daze; my body screaming from exhaustion. All the adrenaline and panic seemed to have seeped out of me, leaving me with no energy.

Despite how tired I felt, I tossed and turned restlessly, unable to fall into the blessing of sleep. Deciding that my brain was too busy for sleep, I got up and picked up a pencil and my sketchbook. I started drawing, adding to the large collection of faces, barely needing to even think about where my hand led the pencil. But it was enough to stop my mind racing with dark thoughts from the day.

When, at last, my eyelids started to droop, I put my sketchbook down, now containing a few extra pages of faces from the night, and tried to fall asleep. This time, only after a few minutes, the peace and calm of sleep started to consume me, and I welcomed it.

•••

I woke up the next morning, seemingly more tired than when I fell asleep. But, despite my aching limbs and heavy eyes, I pulled back the covers and got ready for school.

I was waiting outside the school, standing by the entrance, for George. He told me he'd only be a few minutes, but I hoped he was less than that because the cold was piercing, considerably colder than it had been a few days before. I finally saw him, and at the sight of me, his face lit up. I smiled back at him, no longer caring about the cold.

"Hey, honey, you alright?" he said.

"Better now you're here," I said, not actually answering his question. I really wasn't quite sure. I was glad my parents hadn't flipped out about anything I'd told them, but I was also a little shaken up by everything I'd learnt.

"How are you? Really?"

"Better than I thought I would be. I haven't had a panic attack yet — that's a good sign. I really think it'll be alright," I said, more confidently than I felt. But, as I said it, I started to see the truth in the words.

"I'm glad. How are your parents?"

"Well, my mum said she liked you, so that's good. I haven't spoken to my dad much. I'm not really sure where I stand on my feelings towards him, actually. And, my mum also said she wanted to help me, and she hasn't looked at me like I'm more fragile than a china doll — not yet, anyway," I said.

I could see George's obvious happiness plainly on his face. "Good. And so it should be."

Before I even knew what I was doing, I closed the gap between us and threw my arms around him. I only stayed there for a moment, but when I let go, and before I retreated at all, I gave him a small, quick kiss on his lips.

"Thank you, for everything," I breathed, quieter than I anticipated. I felt like George's close proximity might have had something to do with that.

"You're welcome, sweetie," George whispered.

I glanced at my watch, then, and sighed.

"It's time to go," I said sadly.

We started walking to our tutor rooms, and I gave him another quick hug before he went in and I carried on down the hall.

"Bye."

"Bye."

•••

When we were let out of maths that day, before break, George was waiting outside the door for me. He reached for my hand and led me in the opposite direction from the mainstream flow of students. I followed.

"How was your morning?" he asked, his voice strained in anger. I'd been a little late to maths that day, so we didn't have the chance to speak before the lesson.

"Boring. Yours?" I decided to not ask about his obvious annoyance — not yet, anyway.

"Dull."

"Oh well. Where are we going?" I asked tentatively. I wasn't used to seeing George this way.

"Somewhere quieter."

151

"And where would that be? It's a very busy school." I tried, desperately, to lighten his heavy mood, but it did little to ease him.

"Outside — no one will be there, it's freezing." It was true.

I hated seeing George so wound up and I wondered what had happened to cause it.

We reached the door that led outside and George pushed it open with his free hand. We walked to the picnic benches and sat down.

He didn't say anything, and I started to worry.

"Are you okay?" I asked carefully.

He looked at me, anger and sadness written on his face. He shook his head.

"What's wrong?" I asked gently. When he didn't elaborate, I added, "It might help."

"It's just, in maths, some boys were being really rude," he stopped for a moment and looked into my eyes like he wasn't sure whether or not to carry on. Eventually, after I raised my eyebrows to prompt him, he continued. "They were talking about you. I'm sorry, Zoe. It just makes me so angry. They don't even know how amazing you are, or what you've been through, yet they think it's acceptable to talk about you, behind your back, like you're nothing at all. I had a good mind to punch them."

I squeezed his hand and tried not to think of the worst possible things they could have said. I'd stumbled on an answer in the lesson, and, for once, it hadn't phased me. I hadn't minded, and I didn't freak out. But clearly, other people had picked up on it. I was even in the room; I didn't know how I didn't notice. I swallowed. "It's alright. I'm used to it and it's isn't your fault," I said, desperately trying to cheer him up and not let my sadness show.

"And that's half of the problem. You shouldn't have to be used to it. It should never have gotten so far. You think this is normal, for people to be so mean. But it's not. I wish you'd understand that."

"I know. But it doesn't matter. And, honestly, it doesn't bother me much anymore. Especially now I've got you." I wished he didn't worry about this so much. I'd accepted that people were mean, and that's just how it was. I didn't have to take everything to heart, and it wasn't doing me much harm if I couldn't even hear what they were saying. Sure, the idea stung for a while, but I wouldn't dwell on it for too long or let it get in the way of overcoming my fears. Not anymore.

He looked at me with so much love and pain in his eyes that it broke my heart a little and I resisted the urge to kiss him; the fire burning in yearning.

"I'm sorry," he said, so quietly I had to strain to hear him. He looked utterly defeated and all I wanted to do was hold him in my arms.

"What for?" He didn't have anything to be sorry for.

"For everything. That people treat you so badly and that there's nothing I can do about it, no matter how badly I want to. I wish it weren't the case." He started tracing patterns along my forearm: it calmed me more.

"I know. Me too. But it is, and that's okay. It's not your fault, none of this is," I said shyly.

"We'll get through it together, no matter what." My heart swelled to double its size.

I nodded and smiled, my cheeks burning red. It would be okay. I had George, so whatever was to happen, it wouldn't feel as bad as it would have if I went through it alone.

I gave him a quick kiss on his cheek and laid my head on his shoulder. He stroked my hair softly and it sent small shivers up my spine, but I never would have asked him to stop.

"What will it take for you to understand how perfect you are to me?" George mused after a few minutes of comfortable silence.

"No idea. But keep trying, I'm sure something will work," I said gently.

"Mmm. That's not much to go on. Well, I'll try my best," he said. I laughed at his determination to make me feel better about myself. I stared into his eyes for a minute, and the whole world disappeared, leaving only the two of us.

"You're doing it again," he said, a smile playing at the corner of his lips.

"What?" I asked, bewildered.

"Looking at me like I'm the only person in the room." He played with my hair, and it felt so amazing that I closed my eyes for a little longer than a blink would last, savouring the feeling.

"Well, technically," I said, looking around at the emptiness around us, "you are the only person in the room." We laughed, but then I turned serious. "It's even more than that. I look at you like you're the only person in the world." I confessed, feeling the warmth rush to my cheeks.

"Well, that's even better."

After another five minutes, I glanced at the time and said we should go to our lessons. He nodded reluctantly but stood up nonetheless.

154

We hugged and said goodbye before heading our separate ways to the next lesson.

•••

The bus was still quite empty when I got on at the end of the day and I walked near the back to find my usual seat. I sat down and plugged my earphones in, listening to music, turning the volume up too loud so it was harder to think about what would happen when I got home. I walked home slower than usual, dragging my feet a little, too. My parents worked from home, so there was very little chance of them not being there when I get in.

When I did eventually get home, it was to kind questions about my day. I knew the questions about school could only last so long, and it was just to ease me into the more serious things, but I wished it could last longer than it did. My dad cleared his throat audibly and when I turned to face him, he smiled apologetically. He gestured for me to sit down on one of the sofas and I sat on the other one to both my parents, where George and I sat only the day before.

"We're sorry, Zoe. I know that doesn't even start to cut it after everything we've done. But, we truly are sorry, and we promise, no more secrets. We'll tell you everything from now on and anything you want to tell us, whatever it is, we won't think badly of you. And that applies forever. We just want you to be happy, that's all. So, is there anything else that you want to tell us? You might not have told us everything with George here," my dad said.

I was surprised. I didn't think he'd have it in him to say all that, especially after what happened yesterday. He must have known my feelings towards him were complicated now. I could barely remember which parts I told them yesterday, but, even if I did miss stuff out, I wasn't in the mood to tell them now, anyway.

"Thank you. But don't think I've given up that easily; you made something that was already hard, impossibly harder. But, nonetheless, thank you. And I think I told you everything yesterday," I said, smiling reassuringly at them.

"I know, we're so sorry. And, if there is anything else, you can talk to us anytime. As dad said, we just want you to be happy," my mum said.

I nodded. We sat in awkward silence for a moment. "Anything else?" I asked, desperate to get away from their piercing eyes.

Both my parents shook their heads, so I was free to leave. I smiled at them and then walked out of the room, up the stairs and into my bedroom.

Relief flooded through me, and my mouth automatically pulled up in a smile. My lungs felt like they finally worked properly again; giving me the right amount of oxygen instead of the rationed supply. The only thing that would have made me happier then would have been to have George's arms around me; his lips on mine; his comforting words seeping into my brain. My smile widened, turning into a ridiculous grin. I didn't care if I looked like a Cheshire cat; it was worth it for the magical feeling coursing through my bloodstream. No one could see me, anyway. And, even if they could, I found myself not minding.

24

"Are you doing anything tonight?" I asked George hopefully. We were sitting opposite Emily and Anna at lunch the next week, and it was the first time George was meeting Anna as Emily's girlfriend. It was going amazingly as far as I was concerned, like pieces slotting into place, the four of us laughing and talking freely. A feeling of hope settled within me as I realised this was going to be something that became a regular thing: the four of us eating lunch together and hanging out.

"No, I don't think so. Why?" George asked, confusion knitting his brows together.

"We were thinking of going to the park after school, if you wanted to come?" Emily said. We'd planned on going together anyway, the three of us, and inviting George if that lunchtime went well.

"You do know it's November, right? In England?" George asked dubiously. We'd already had to resort to eating inside in the canteen because of the cold. None of us wanted to leave our private lunch space, but we'd been shivering so badly we could barely hold our sandwiches and our fingers were numb by the end of lunch. We'd had to give in to the weather eventually.

And I wasn't scared to sit in the canteen anymore, not with George and Emily – and now Anna – by my side. I felt protected from the potential of the smirks and degrading comments from Jane and her seemingly ginormous friend group.

"There's an indoor café," Anna added.

"Exactly. We won't freeze to death," Emily agreed.

George laughed a little, then said, "Sure."

We arranged the details as he texted his parents to get permission, and a flutter of excitement bloomed in my chest at the idea of spending more time with the three of them.

•••

Sitting at the circle table in the café in the park, the four of us huddled around a table really meant for two, sipping a hot chocolate, I couldn't stop smiling. I felt so, so unbelievably happy in that moment, surrounded by people who made me laugh so much I cried and who made me not care about what I looked like, or how I acted. Because I could just be myself and that was more than enough for them.

I felt at home; like I'd been waiting my whole life to become friends with George, Emily and Anna and I'd finally found the people I was destined to be with. Not that I believed in fate. I believed we made our own choices and we had the power to change our own lives. But that didn't mean I wasn't aware of how I felt like this was meant to be, and somehow we were supposed to find each other.

Our laughter filled the almost empty room, and the waitress looked at us in slightly bewildered contempt, like laughter was something she wasn't used to. But I didn't care; I was having way too much fun.

When it was almost time to leave, we put our mugs on the counter, and collected our bags, heading out into the unforgiving cold. The clouds above our heads looked black, and I hoped it wouldn't start to rain until I'd gotten home. I hated the rain.

However, only a few seconds later, the heavens opened and rain started pattering on the ground, quickly escalating into a downpour, in true English style. We all ducked back underneath the awning, laughing as the rain splashed us.

I stepped back and somehow George was behind me, his arms wrapping around me, and I threw my head back, resting it again this chest as I laughed. I noticed that Emily was reaching for Anna's hand, and I smiled, feeling genuinely happy for the two of them.

I twisted around in George's arm and stood on my toes, pressing my lips to his as I brought his head to mine, my fingers trapping his hair in my hands. Everything felt so right, so natural, and I smiled when we pulled back, unable to contain my happiness.

"What?" George asked, smiling too.

I shook my head. "I'm just really happy," I said truthfully.

"Me too," he said, and I twisted back around in his arms so my back was pressed against his front.

We untangled, and we all walked to the other end of the cover so we could at least see the car park when our parents turned up in a few minutes. Yet again, I wished we could drive, but for now, we'd have to rely on the parent taxi.

Anna's dad came first, and she hugged us all, only hugging Emily for slightly longer, but in a way that you wouldn't suspect they were anything more than friends. I knew then that she still wasn't out to her parents, and my heart reached out to her. I hoped she'd find the courage soon.

My mum came shortly after, and we were dropping Emily off too, so we said goodbye to George, me giving him a quick kiss before jogging to the car in the rain, trying to stay as dry as possible. I ran around to the other side to let Emily get in first, then slipped in, quickly slamming the door behind me to keep the worst of the rain out.

"Hello, you two," my mum said cheerfully from the front, as we buckled in and she started driving away. "You have a good day?"

We passed George's mums car, but I couldn't see in because of the rain pounding against the windshield. I never seemed to be able to catch a glimpse of her. I guessed I'd have to wait until the weekend when I went over to his house to meet his parents. The idea terrified me, but I tried to not agonise over it too much.

"Yeah, we did," I said, really meaning it. I smiled over at Emily to find her smiling right back. I wanted to ask about Anna, but I knew I'd have to wait until tomorrow when we were alone.

We chatted for the rest of the journey to her house, then we said goodbye and I moved into the passenger seat before we drove off again.

"You look happy," my mum said mischievously.

I felt heat rush to my cheeks, but I was smiling. "Yeah. I'm really happy," I said. And before I lost the guts, I carried on. "I feel like I've found somewhere I

160

belong. It's just so natural and I feel carefree and it's easy to be with them; I haven't had that before. So yeah. I'm happy."

I looked over at my mum, and she was smiling. "Good. I'm glad, darling," she said, reaching for my hand across the seats and giving it a quick squeeze before returning it to the wheel.

And that small gesture made my happiness expand tenfold.

25

I smoothed down my skirt, taking deep breaths before heading downstairs to go to George's house. I was nervous, but not awfully so, and I believed that with some conscious effort to keep calm, I'd be able to get through the day: I was meeting George's parents for lunch.

My mum drove me, and we sat in silence for most of the journey, music from the radio filling the quiet. When we pulled up to the house, I marvelled again at the beautiful collection of flowers, appreciating all the shades of colours painted there which was much more beautiful in daylight.

I thanked my mum, reminding her of the plan of when to pick me up, and I stepped out of the car gingerly. I walked up the path on slightly unsteady legs and knocked on the door, hoping I was only imagining my shaking hands.

After only a few seconds, it opened. Standing in the doorway was a lady — forty or so years old — with auburn brown hair, falling just below her shoulders in loose waves. She smiled warmly at me, showing perfect white teeth. Her eyes were a soft green, lined with long lashes, but they'd been thinned over the years. She wore a simple white blouse with a burgundy skater skirt which showed off her stunning figure perfectly.

"Hello. You must be Zoe. Nice to meet you," she said kindly, offering me her hand to shake. Her voice vaguely reminded me of wind chimes, despite there being very little similarity. I pushed down my fear and shook her hand gently.

"Nice to meet you, too," I said, hoping only I could hear the vague wobble.

"Come on in out of the cold," she said, opening the door wider and stepping aside. Despite my nerves, I was grateful to get out of the biting air. As I passed George's mum, I thanked her.

There were pictures lining the hall, and I smiled at pictures of George as a baby. George stepped out of a room which I assumed was the dining room, from the table I could see through the open door, and he smiled when he saw me.

"Hey, you," he said, coming over to give me a hug.

"Hi." With his arms around me, I instantly felt more at ease. I realised I'd been stupid to worry so much: his mum had already been kind, and I doubted his dad would act any differently.

We pulled apart and his mum smiled at us, then she led us through to a living room with a slowly diminishing fire in the fireplace. It was warm and cosy and the sofas were a soft cream colour, adding to the comfort. On one of the sofas sat a man with short-cropped black hair and a stubble-covered chin. His eyes were a soft brown and when he looked up from his newspaper, he smiled at us all. His parents held little resemblance to George, but his father had the same strong jaw as George, and his smile mirrored his mother's.

"Mum, Dad, this is Zoe," George said gesturing to me, despite it being quite unnecessary. "Zoe, this is my mum, Sue, and my dad, Jeff."

"Hello," I said smiling. I was desperately hoping my facade was good enough to fool them I was comfortable and not worried at all. I wondered briefly whether George had told them about my anxiety, trying to minimise the chance that they'd set off an attack. I couldn't help but wonder how much they knew about me.

"Sit, sit," George's mum said. George reached for my hand and sat down on the nearest sofa, pulling me down with him.

"So, tell us about yourself. George hasn't told us as much as I'd like to know," Sue said, smiling at me and then glancing disapprovingly at George. He rolled his eyes.

My stomach churned uncomfortably. I hated these questions; I never knew what I was supposed to say. "Er, I don't know. There isn't much to tell," I said vaguely.

"Nonsense!" she insisted.

"Okay. Um...what do you want to know?" I asked, deeming it safer to go down this route.

I squeezed George's hand, seeking comfort, and took a deep breath, hoping it wasn't noticeable.

"Hobbies?" she suggests tentatively.

"I do trampolining and I really love art," I said.

"Do you compete?" she prompted, smiling encouragingly.

"No. I only do it at the school club. But I'd like to; my parents won't let me, though," I said, sighing. I felt a bit more comfortable now; my stomach churning less.

"Oh, that's a shame," Sue said. I nodded, already lost for more to say.

Thankfully, George stepped in. "Zoe's working on an art project, aren't you?" He was smiling wide, and I knew he was remembering, as I was, the night I talked for almost fifteen minutes without interruption about my project and he'd made me feel like I was all he wanted. The thought made me smile.

"Um, yeah. I'm doing loads of faces, all in different materials, and with different emotions and I'm trying to show how not everything is as it seems, and people don't always show what they're feeling and…" I trailed off, suddenly embarrassed by how much I'd said.

"Go on," Jeff said encouragingly, smiling. Sue nodded too, and George smiled. He knew what I was going to say next.

"And how you don't have to hide your emotions because you're not alone," I finished. I blushed, realising what I'd said and how that may all come across as strange to my boyfriend's parents.

But they didn't seem to think so. Both Sue and Jeff were smiling at me, with a strange kind of admiration in their eyes, and I felt my blush deepen. "I'd like to see these one day," Sue said. I nodded, grateful that they took my ramblings well.

We talked a little more, getting to know each other a little, and then after a few minutes, George said, "Dad, can you help me get the lunch ready?" He nodded his head to the door, and panic suddenly flooded through me. He couldn't leave me alone, I needed him there.

He saw the panic on my face quickly and I shook my head at him slightly, but firmly. He mouthed that I'd be fine, then he squeezed my hand and he was gone, leaving just me and Sue in the room. I got the sense that this was engineered that I'd be alone with Sue and that only made my nerves jangle even more.

Sue stood up and walked over to the sofa that I was sitting on. She sat down gracefully and placed a hand on my knee, looking at me and smiling, doing a poor job of reassuring me.

"Listen, Zoe. George has told us about your anxiety," she paused there, and I instantly felt anxious, dreading what she'd say. It didn't shock me, though. I was almost suspecting it. "And, believe it or not, I used to suffer from dreadful anxiety. George was wondering if I could give you some tips." I nodded at her, bewildered that a woman who looked so confident now, used to be like me. It gave me a flickering hope. Maybe I would be alright, I thought.

"Do you mind telling me a bit about your anxiety? It will help me to help you," she said gently.

I took a deep breath, then told her most of it. It's for the best, anyway. I felt comfortable talking to Sue, despite my initial doubts. I guess the knowledge that she understood what I felt was reassuring. She didn't say anything until I'd finished and, even then, she stayed quiet for a moment, her brows furrowed.

"I'm sorry to hear that, love. No one should have to go through all that at such a young age. Have you had any help before? Or told anyone?" she said kindly.

"Not really. I only told my parents the other week, when George came to mine, and George was the only other person I've told properly. Emily knows some too,

166

but not all of it," I said. Then, before I could change my mind, I said, "George really has been amazing. Honestly, he's a miracle. It's like I've won the lottery. He's helped me so much with everything, especially my self-esteem, confidence and anxiety. I just wanted you to know."

She smiled at me again, seemingly very appreciative of my words, but being unable to form the words she wanted to say to me. Instead, she just nodded in thanks.

"Right, back to tips." She gave me some simple breathing exercises to help and some self-appreciation things too. She told me more about the science behind anxiety and panic attacks and gave me some things to think of to try and calm myself. I wrote it all down on a bit of paper she handed me, so I didn't forget anything, because most of it seemed like it might help and I gave her my email so she could send over some more information. After all, it was worth a try.

"Remember, I'm always here if you want to talk, I'd be happy to help. And, Zoe, you are a wonderful girl, don't let other people tell you otherwise. George is lucky to have you, and he really does care for you greatly. You seem like the type of girl that doesn't believe him when he tells you. But, he's been so much happier recently, because of you. You are someone special, I promise," she said once she finished giving advice.

She took my hand in hers. I wanted to believe every word she said, and I did — a little. I was starting to believe that compliments were true, at last. George would have been happy for me, and I had him to thank for it. I nodded at Sue, saying more with the gesture and my eyes than words could convey.

At that moment George and Jeff walked in and I jumped a little at the sound of them, letting go of Sue's hand.

"Lunch is ready," George said cheerfully. He had a mischievous glint in his eyes, and I wondered if they really had gone to prepare lunch or if it was simply an excuse to leave us alone. Either way, I was actually glad for it. I was grateful that Sue was so willing to help me and how much she gave me to work through.

I smiled up at him, and looked at the paper in my hands, before folding it up and slipping it into my pocket. I stood up and walked over to George, who took my hand and led me into the dining room. All the food was already set out on the table, salad leaves and a variety of cured meats and cheeses which looked simple but delicious. George pulled out a chair for me, and I slid in as everyone else took their seats at the table.

"This looks lovely," I said politely.

"Thank you. Help yourself," Sue said, and George started filling his plate, so I did the same. We talked more, and after a short while, I felt more and more at ease, the words becoming easier to say and the laughs coming more naturally. Sue and Jeff were lovely to me, kind and easy-going and I was glad that they seemed to like me and accept me as their son's girlfriend.

By the time we'd finished the pudding, I felt almost completely comfortable and I wondered why I'd stressed so much beforehand. I hoped I'd see much more of the inside of this house.

"Thank you for lunch," I said again, before George and I left the room to head up to his bedroom for a while before my mum picked me up.

"No problem," Sue said, and Jeff nodded. They both smiled at us before we went out and I followed George up the stairs.

We got to his bedroom, and I tried to hide a gasp. Along one of the walls were several guitars all hung up, and there was sheet music completely covering the same wall. The other walls were less remarkable, painted a modern grey colour, with a bookcase full of books and shelves with photos, CDs and DVDs on. The bed was made, and there was a blue blanket covering the duvet. The whole room was so George, I couldn't help but smile.

He took my hand and pulled me down to the floor with him, I lay down, resting my head in his lap as he leant against the wall. He ran his fingers through my hair, twisting strands around his fingers.

"You didn't mind me telling them, did you?" George asked hesitantly.

I shook my head. "No. It really helped, actually, what your mum said. Could you thank her for me? I know it must have been hard for her."

"Good. I'm glad. And, of course, I will. Really, I don't think she minds that much anymore, especially if it helps you." I looked up at him, and he was smiling. "They like you, by the way. Especially my mum."

The corners of my mouth curled up; I was happy they approved of me.

In that moment, a spiral of feeling washed through me, and I suddenly had a perfect word for what I felt towards George. I looked up at him. I hesitated for just a moment before opening my mouth. "I love you, George," I said, my heart racing.

His face broke into a smile, and the small amount of nerves from saying that for the first time dissolved. "I love you, too," he said gently, and I could hear the love in his voice.

My heart swelled yet again.

We talked more until my phone pinged. I reached around George to get my phone off the shelve I left it on, and I sighed. "My mums here," I said.

He sighed too. It didn't matter that we'd talk later and see each other the day after tomorrow at school – it still meant leaving him, even momentarily. I stood up, and George took my hand again and led me out of the room and down the stairs.

We walked back into the lounge to find Sue and Jeff sitting on the sofa.

"Thank you so much for having me," I said. "My mums here now."

"It was a pleasure. You're welcome here whenever you like," Sue said, smiling up at me.

"Thank you again," I said, looking at Sue, hoping she knew what I meant. She nodded and I smiled again.

"It was lovely to meet you, Zoe," Jeff said approvingly.

"You too," I said.

Just before I walked through the doorway, I bade Sue and Jeff goodbye, giving them a little wave.

George and I were alone in the hall, and I rose on my toes and gently pressed my lips to his. Both our lips were smiling and I wanted to stay like that forever, encased in the glorious presence of George. With him pressed so close to me, I could easily forget about all my worries. Fire burned at the contact our lips made, and I wanted to ignite the fire further, but being consciously

170

aware of the company in the next room, I grudgingly fell back after a too-short length of time.

"Bye," I breathed in his ear.

"Bye. I'll miss you."

"I'll miss you more. I'll text you when I get home."

I quickly flung my arms around his neck and pressed my body close to his, savouring how amazingly good it felt to be so close to this wonderful boy.

But, after just a few seconds, I turned on my heel reluctantly and walked through the door, wishing I could still be in George's arms as I walked down the path, waving to my mum in the car. I turned before I stepped in, and George was leaning against the doorframe, smiling at me. I felt warmth course through me at the sight of him and I felt, once again, truly happy.

26

"Zoe, can we talk?" My dad was standing in the doorway of my room, his hand awkwardly holding the frame as he waited for my response. My mum had gone out to do the shopping, leaving us alone in the house.

"Yeah, ok," I said, putting down my charcoal and wiping my fingers on a piece of kitchen roll in an attempt to get rid of the black staining them. My dad walked in and sat down on my bed as I twisted around in my chair to face him. I tried not to let the rising panic show on my face. I had a good idea of what he wanted to talk about, and I wasn't sure if I was ready. It had been a few weeks since I'd found out about Rob, and I still didn't know where I sat on it.

I looked at my dad as I waited for him to say something, and he looked embarrassed, and I realised this was worse for him than it was for me. But he was the one who'd made the mistake, and he deserved to feel a little uncomfortable.

He looked at me, not quite in my eyes but not far off, and finally, he spoke. "I'm sorry I didn't tell you about Rob and I'm sorry it happened. But I need you to know that nothing like that has happened again, and it never will. I would never hurt your mother or you or Grace like that again. I promise you."

He swallowed, but I didn't say anything yet, sensing he had more to say. "I know you may not trust me at the moment, and your feelings may be a bit conflicted, and I'm sorry about that. I understand that this may take a little while for you to fully grasp, and that's ok. But I'll always be here for you, Zoe. I promise."

Shifting on the bed, my dad clasped his hands together in his lap. I thought about how I felt towards him, how much he'd hurt my mum and the other woman, Marian. How much he'd hurt his son. I thought about how he seemed sorry, and I wanted to believe him when he said he'd never do it again.

Finally, I swallowed. "How can I know you're not lying?"

My dad stayed silent for a moment, then he looked me in the eyes and I felt oddly exposed like he could see straight through me, see my hurt and confusion bright as day. "I haven't left you."

I stared back at him, unsure what to say. But before I could try and string together a sentence, he carried on. "Before you started secondary school, do you remember what you said to me?" I shook my head. "You said, 'Dad, I'm scared.' And I told you that I'd always protect you so you'd never have to feel scared. And I stand by that. I love you so, so much, Zoe. I made a horrible mistake, and I've learnt from it."

"Did you make mum stay with you?" I whispered. I wasn't sure if I wanted to know the answer, but I think I needed to.

"I let her decide. Obviously, I would have been devastated had she chosen differently, but I would have understood. I love her, and if that meant letting her go because of my mistake, then so be it. But I'm glad she didn't leave me," he said. His voice held a wistful tone to it, and somehow I knew I'd forgive him, in time.

"Ok," I said simply. I didn't know what else to say. My dad nodded.

"If there's ever anything else you want to know or want to say, I'll answer and I'll listen. I won't keep anything else from you, Zoe."

"Ok," I said again.

"Good." My dad stood, about to walk out.

"Can I meet Rob? Properly, this time," I said quickly, before he could leave. I wanted to get to know my brother, at least a little. It wasn't his fault, what happened.

"If that's what you want, then yes," my dad said after a beat.

"It's what I want."

"Ok, I'll try and get his number for you, and you can chat," he said, nodding his head. I didn't know how he was going to do it, but that was his problem. He needed to prove to me that he was serious about everything he'd said.

"Thanks," I said.

He started walking again, and as he passed me, he pressed a hand to my shoulder. It was an oddly formal gesture for him: my dad was more into the half-hugs. But the slightly more distant gesture comforted me, like he was giving me space to come to terms with everything. I smiled up at him before he left the room, leaving me staring at the door after him.

•••

174

It was a few hours later when my dad came back into my room, a small piece of paper in his hand. I was sitting on my bed with a book in my hand, music playing out of my speakers. My phone sat next to me, and I'd only just gotten off the phone with George, telling him about what had happened with my dad earlier.

"Here," my dad said, reaching out his hand to me. I put down my book and took the paper from between his fingers, and on it was a mobile phone number, scrawled in my dad's uneven handwriting. "That's Rob's number."

"Thank you," I said, meaning it. I smiled at him, then he left the room without another word, his footsteps retreating down the stairs.

I stared at the numbers for a moment before grabbing my phone and typing them in under a new contact for Rob. I opened up a new message and started writing out a text, typing and deleting and typing again until I'd finally written something I was happy with. I took a deep breath before hitting send, not knowing what would happen because of it.

Zoe: Hi, Rob. It's Zoe Rose. I hope you don't mind me getting in contact, but I wanted to meet you, properly this time. I'm sorry about last time. But I know now, and I'd like to see you again so we can talk. Let me know if that's something you'd be interested in. Thanks

I went back to reading, but after barely five minutes my phone pinged.

Rob: Ok. When?

I breathed out a sigh of relief and typed out an answer.

Zoe: How about tomorrow at break? Meet at the beginning of break beneath the green canopy?

Rob: Sure. See you then

•••

The next day, as soon as I was let out of art, I said goodbye to Emily and Anna and made my way down to the green canopy. I figured it would be private, but not too private, and Rob would know where it was, even if he hadn't been at the school very long.

I hadn't planned anything to say, but I hoped I'd know when I saw him.

I got there before Rob, but I only had to wait about a minute before I saw him round the corner and walk towards me. A small jolt went through me at the sight of him. He was my brother. My brother. The word sounded strange in my head.

I tried to calm my racing heart. The uncertainty of how this would turn out was a little daunting.

"Hi," I said when he came close enough to talk at a normal volume. I smiled at him, hoping to show I wanted to be kind.

"Hey," he said, smiling. Relief flooded through me. He sounded a little nervous, but the anger and confusion and hurt from last time were gone.

We stayed standing, but I didn't mind. I struggled for something to say, but Rob spoke first.

"I'm really sorry about last time. I shouldn't have done that, even if you had known. I was angry and upset and I shouldn't have taken it out on you like that. I just thought you knew..." he trailed off, probably remembering that day, like I was: his repeated apology and the manic, confused look in his eyes. I twisted the ring around my finger, giving me something to focus on. It was a silver band, with a gold heart in the middle.

"It's ok. I would have been angry had it been me. But I didn't know. I asked my parents about it that day, and they told me. I'm sorry it worked out the way it did. But, for the record, if I'd known about you, I would have tried to get in contact somehow," I said, hoping to convey how I felt.

"Thanks, that means a lot. I just assumed you'd know, but I guess it makes more sense that your parents wouldn't tell you. I hope I haven't ruined anything for you," he said, sounding guilty.

I shook my head. "No, you haven't. I haven't forgiven my dad yet, but maybe I will soon. He hurt my mum a lot, that's all," I said, wincing slightly. "Our dad. Sorry, I'm still not used to this."

He smiled awkwardly. "That's ok. I've had a while to get used to it."

I hesitated, then spoke anyway. "Are you angry at me?"

He smiled, shaking his head. "No, not now. I thought you were ignoring me on purpose, before, but obviously, you weren't. I'm not angry at you."

"Who are you angry at?" I asked, though I think I knew the answer.

"My parents, I guess. My mum, for taking me away from our dad. She could have stayed in England and he'd be a part of my life, you all would be. But she wouldn't have that. And our dad. I'm not even quite sure why…" he trailed off again. I didn't know what to say, so instead, I nodded.

We lapsed into an awkward silence, years of secrets and unfamiliarity stopping our words. Finally, I thought of something. "I'd like to get to know you, Rob. Become a sister to you," I said hopefully.

He smiled, wider than I'd seen on him. "I'd like that. I can finally be a brother."

Beaming, I tentatively reached out my arms, suggesting a hug. He shrugged, then stepped forward. We hugged, quickly. But it was enough to make me believe that we could become close, that we'd see more of each other and I'd have a brother.

27

Reaching over my sketchbook, the page full of swirling colours, in a vague shape of a disfigured face, I grabbed my phone and rang George. Band practice had finished by now.

He picked up after three rings. "Hello, beautiful," he said.

"Hey. How was band practice?" I asked, smiling wider than I already was at the sound of his voice

"Great. We finished that piece we've been working on, at last," he said, clearly proud of himself and the band. He should have been proud. I'd heard him play and he was extremely talented. I was surprised there was any talent left for anyone else, with the amount he used up. He could play almost all instruments, but his favourite was an acoustic guitar.

"Well done," I said, "will I get to hear this piece?"

"Um, yeah sure. We could do it tomorrow at break if you wanted?" he asked, sounding a bit nervous.

"Yes! I'd love that. You'll be amazing, don't worry," I said, looking forward to hearing him play again. He didn't like me listening because he worried I wouldn't like it, which was utterly ridiculous.

"Thanks. So, how are you?" he asked.

"Good. I'm actually pretty happy right now." I was smiling, and I guessed he could hear the smile in my voice.

"And why's that exactly?" he asked sceptically.

"Because of you. Why else?" I said teasingly.

"I'm happy I make you happy. And, for the record, you make me immensely happy, too."

"Well, thank God for that," I laughed. "Not that I know why, really. You deserve much better than me, George," I said slowly, my smile lessening slightly. I didn't really mean to throw a damper on things, but I couldn't help it. I felt I could be completely honest with him, and the idea was nagging at me.

"No, Zoe. Don't ever think that. You deserve the kindest and sweetest guy in the world and I don't deserve someone as wonderful as you. You're better than anyone else, I promise," he said, kindly but with obvious sternness as well.

"I've already got the kindest and sweetest guy in the world, whether I deserve it or not is a different matter. But, thank you anyway." My heart swelled at his words and I couldn't believe how lucky I was to have George.

"Thank you, darling. My mum's here to pick me up now, so I've got to go. Bye, Zoe. I love you," he said.

I sighed. "Bye, George. I love you, too." Then I hung up and went back to my art, the disfigured faces taking on a twisted smile.

•••

George took my hand and led us to the music practice room his band always used. I'd met him outside my history class, and, for once, he'd been the nervous one. Apparently, our roles had been reversed.

He pushed the door open and said, "Hi, guys, this is Zoe."

I smiled at them all — there were only three others — and they all said various versions of greetings and smiled at me. I'd never met any of George's friends, at least not officially, but I knew his bandmates were his closest friends. I hoped they'd like me.

"Any friend of George is a friend of ours," Tom, the drummer, said to me.

"That is, of course, providing you treat him well," Dan, the bassist, added, laughing.

"Don't worry," I said, joking along. There was no chance I'd ever treat George badly; I couldn't. I didn't want to say that, though.

"I don't think you need to worry about that, she treats me great," George said, throwing his arm around my shoulders and bringing me closer to him.

"Thanks," I said, looking up to see him.

"No problem. It's true, too." He gave me a quick kiss on the lips and my breath caught. I didn't think he'd kiss me in front of his friends like that, at least not within the first three minutes.

I quickly looked away and instantly blushed when I realised Tom, Dan and Bradley, the pianist, were looking at us with smiles plastered on their faces.

"Zoe, you're blushing," Dan said, laughing a little. I could tell he wasn't making fun of me, but I still wished he hadn't said it.

"I know, it's cute, isn't it?" George mused, which only made my blush deeper. I bit my lip.

"No need to be embarrassed, Zoe. We're all happy for you two, you're as cute as anything together," Bradley said, joining in. I smiled sheepishly.

I liked George's bandmates. They seemed genuinely kind and I had a good feeling about them like this would be a place where I wouldn't be judged.

"Honestly, they like you, they're all glad I've got someone like you," George whispered into my hair, sending goose-bumps along my arms.

I nodded discreetly, hoping only George noticed.

"I came here to hear your song, so can I hear it now, please?" I asked, desperately trying to get the attention off me.

"Sure, we just need to set George up, then we'll be ready to go," Tom said, flashing me a smile.

"You," George said, taking my hand and leading me to a chair, "sit here and enjoy." I sat and he kissed the top of my head before going to set up his guitar.

After a minute, they all nodded at each other, confirming they were ready, I presumed, and then Tom started on the drums. He played slowly and then the piano started, then bass, then, finally George on guitar. As soon as George started playing, I put all my focus into his fingers dancing along the strings and the way it sounded: calm, relaxing and full of admiration. The music progressed into a faster beat and then came back down again; until it became so slow it faded away entirely, leaving George to play the last note, letting it drag on until the room was filled with silence.

It was one of the most lovely songs I'd ever heard and I wanted them to play it again so the beautiful rhythm could vibrate the floor again, filling the whole room with the beat of the lovely music.

George set down his guitar and walked over to me while I blinked back the tears starting to well up in my eyes. He took my hand and pulled me up, looking into my eyes.

"And that, my beautiful girl, was inspired by you," George said. It took a moment for that to sink in. But when it did, I smiled so wide and stupidly that he chuckled.

"You like it?" he asked nervously.

"Did I like it? Of course, I liked it, I loved it, thank you," I squealed. I couldn't hide my delight. I had to blink back tears again because the notes still ringing in my ears held a whole new meaning now.

"Good."

He kissed me again, but this time for longer and I wrapped my arms around his neck, keeping him close to me. I pulled back, suddenly remembering our company. I blushed again, even though they were all pretending to be busy doing something.

"You guys really wrote that?" I asked, bewildered.

"Yeah. Well, George wrote his bit and then we just developed it together. That's what we normally do," Dan said, smirking at us.

"You never told me you wrote the songs," I said, looking at George, with my eyebrows raised. I was certain I was looking at him with so much admiration in my eyes that I probably shocked him.

"I didn't want to brag," he said sheepishly.

"I love hearing you brag. It makes me realise how much luckier I am to have you," I said, rubbing my thumb on his hand.

"Okay, then, I'll remember to brag all the time then," he said laughing softly.

"Maybe not all the time, it will get very annoying," I said, laughing a bit too.

"I was only joking, honey," he said, using his thumb to softly stroke my cheek.

"I know."

He kissed me gently on the lips again, but only for a second before pulling away.

That time, when I looked over his shoulder, the boys barely averted their eyes in time, and I caught Bradley looking at us seemingly very happily. I didn't blush as much that time, but heat still rushed to my cheeks.

"We need to go to lessons," I said sadly.

They all grunted in agreement.

"You guys were all so amazing; you must work really hard," I complimented.

"Thanks, glad you enjoyed it," Tom said.

"It was quite nice having an audience for once, you should come more often," Bradley said. I nodded and smiled at them all and then hugged George tightly. His next lesson was just next door, so I had to leave before him.

"Bye, my lovely girl," George said just before I opened the door.

"Bye, my musician," I said, looking over my shoulder.

He blew me a kiss and then I walked out, leaving George and his friends, who seemed amazing, behind me.

I closed the door softly and heard the faint click.

Just as I was about to walk away, I heard Bradley's muffled voice. "Dude, you're hopelessly in love."

184

"I know," George's quiet voice replied. I peeked through the little window, being careful not to be seen. I shouldn't have stayed to eavesdrop, but I couldn't help it. I seemed unable to turn around and walk away.

"She seems great. You're lucky as hell," Bradley told him.

"I know. I just wish she would understand, too," George sighed.

"She'll come around, I promise. Anyway, with you being the romantic that you are, it shouldn't take long for her to realise," Bradley said, placing his hand on George's shoulder.

"I hope so. As long as she knows I care, it'll be alright," George said, smiling at Bradley.

"Zoe's cool. And pretty," Tom said, joining in the discussion about me.

"She's not pretty, she's stunning," George replied. "And mine." George looked pointedly towards Tom.

"I know, mate. I would never even think of taking her from you," Tom said.

"How did you get so lucky, dude? She's great," Dan said, joining in, too.

"Well, I'm glad you all like her. I think she likes you guys, too," George said, smiling despite himself.

"We'll be seeing more of her, yeah? I want us all to be friends," Bradley said excitedly.

"I hope so. I'll talk to her about it. I'm sure she'll be fine; she might just need a bit of getting used to it. She's not all that great with confidence," George said.

"We'll make her feel welcome, I promise," Dan said. George nodded gratefully.

"As much as I love talking about Zoe, we've got to go to class," said Tom.

Someone grumbled in agreement and then they finished packing away. I quickly walked in the direction of my class and smiled so wide that a few younger students looked at me a little longer than they should have. I didn't care, though. What George just said about me made all my insides turn warm and fuzzy, like the heating had been turned up. No one had ever said anything about me that made me feel so amazing before. I was so unbelievably happy that his friends liked me, too. I'd be glad to become friends with George's friends, they all seemed so kind and down to earth, and I didn't even feel anxious around them. It's like I'd accepted them subconsciously.

By the time I got to my classroom, my smile was still wider than the ocean. I tried to lessen it because I didn't want to look this ecstatic when coming into a lesson. It worked, for a minute, until it crept onto my face again and I didn't try to hide it that time.

"You look happy," Emily said, a smile playing at her lips. She playfully nudged my shoulder as I unzipped my bag. I didn't take anything out, though, just turned towards her, the smile on my face impossibly wider at the sight of her.

I nodded. "I am. I'm really happy," I said. Then for no other reason other than I wanted to, I wrapped my arms around her in a hug. She squealed in surprise and I couldn't help but laugh. Before I knew it, we were both in hysterics, throwing our heads back in uncontrollable laughter and happiness.

I didn't care what I looked like. I wanted people to know I was happy.

I was done hiding.

Epilogue — Six Months Later

"Zoe, he's here," my mum shouted up the stairs.

"Coming," I yelled back, even though it wasn't strictly true: I wasn't ready yet. George was ten minutes early.

But, because I didn't want to lose even a second of potential time with George, I quickly ran a brush through my hair, creating a side parting faster than I'd ever done before. Hurrying with the final touches of my makeup, I smiled. I'd smiled a lot in the last half-year. Not the fake smile that I'd become accustomed to, but a genuine smile. A smile that, no matter how hard I tried, I couldn't suppress.

Once I'd finished, I ran down the stairs and fell into George's waiting arms.

"You're early," I commented.

"Sorry, but I couldn't wait another minute to see you," George replied, stroking my hair softly.

He pulled back and quickly kissed me. Every single time our lips touched, fire burned deep in my veins, waiting for the moment it could take over. Almost every time he so much as touched my skin, my breath caught. I would have thought that, by now, I wouldn't have been reacting so drastically. But, the electric current never lessened and the fire continued to be fuelled.

He lightly ran his hand down my arm and took my hand in his.

"She'll be back by ten, I promise," George said, turning his head towards my mum and flashing her a smile, always the example of a perfect boyfriend. Almost twelve hours with George, I thought, feeling excitement rush through me.

My mum smiled and nodded at him. "Alright, you kids have fun," my mum said, waving us out of the door.

"You ready?" George asked after my mum closed the door behind us and we walked down the path.

"Yep. You going to tell me what we're doing?" I asked sceptically. Today was supposed to be a surprise, and he'd done a good job at keeping it that way. He shook his head, smiling at me.

"Where we're going?" I asked hopefully, raising my eyebrows.

"Nope."

"You can be stubborn, can't you?" I mused.

"I sure can. I know you love it really," he said, opening the car door for me. I slid in and he softly clicked the door shut, before walking around to the other side to get in himself. Sue sat in the driver's seat, tapping her fingers against the steering wheel.

"Good morning, Zoe. How are you?" She asked me, turning her head towards me.

"Really good, thanks," I replied, trying to convey that I wasn't just talking about how I was feeling then, but how I felt in general.

"Good, I'm glad," she said, a smile playing at her lips. I smiled and nodded my head.

"Strap in, you two," Sue said.

I put on my seatbelt and placed my hand in between where George and I were sitting. Barely half a second later he closed his hand around mine, a smug smile on his face.

Thoughts of my life before George came flooding back to me and it hit me like a bomb: the loneliness before him; the endless worrying; the lack of confidence and, most importantly, the anxiety that haunted my life. But, now, it was like I was a completely different person. My worries were almost always calmed when George was with me or talked to me, and my confidence had risen tenfold. I didn't know how he did it, but, without me even realising, I wasn't an unconfident wreck anymore. Anxiety still lingered in the corners of my life, taunting me whenever it pleased, but it wasn't as bad. Sue helped massively with that, and she almost became my counsellor and my therapist to help me through my anxiety. She became another mother to me, and I was eternally grateful to her because of it.

I thought of my mental list I'd created all those months ago of all the things I would do if only I had the confidence to do them and I felt oddly proud of myself. Because I felt I'd achieved a lot of the things I wanted to. I'd plucked up the courage to tell George how I really felt, I'd spoken up in class more and made more friends, doing more things besides going to school. The fear that had weighed me down constantly now only appeared every now and again and, miraculously, I felt at ease in my skin.

Glancing at mine and George's hands, I smiled — because I won the ultimate lottery prize.

•••

Every other minute, I gazed out of the window, trying to determine where we were headed, but with no success. I recognised where we were, but I couldn't work out any more than that.

After what felt like an eternity of driving, Sue pulled up into a park that I hadn't heard of before.

"We're here, my love," George squealed, squeezing my hand in anticipation.

"I still don't know what we're doing, though," I said exaggeratedly. He laughed.

"The best is yet to come."

I beamed at him. He let go of my hand, which caused it to fall limply on the seat between us, and he opened his door to slide out. I did the same but was startled when I saw George standing right outside my door, hand on the handle, his eyebrows furrowed, but twitching as they fought to rise to their normal position.

"What?" I asked, suppressing the urge to burst out into hysterical laughter.

"I wanted to be gentlemanly today, and that involved opening your door for you," he said, gesturing to the door like I might need a reminder as to what one is.

"You don't have to do that for me, you know," I teased.

"Well, I'm going to do it whether you like it or not," George said, his voice cracking with the strain of not laughing.

"I'll be good, I promise," I said, giving in to the giggles building up inside me.

"Good," he replied, a smile creeping onto his face.

"You two enjoy yourselves, okay? I'll pick you up at nine-thirty," Sue said cheerfully through the open window.

"Thank you," George told her. Something about the way he tilted his head and shifted his eyes made me think there was more to it than a simple appreciation.

I smiled warmly at Sue and watched the silver car drive away, waiting for the blissful moment when we'd be totally alone.

"Ready for the best day of your life?" George asked, holding my hand loosely.

"Of course, I am," I said. Rising to my toes, I kissed his nose gently, before moving onto his lips. He had no idea how ready I was for this.

•••

"Do you want to know something?" I asked George, turning my head up to face him. The path we walked on twisted through a stunning park, lined on each side by a beautiful array of trees, each sporting a different coloured blossom. The tarmac beneath us was smooth, meaning I could focus my whole attention on George.

"Of course. You can tell me anything," he replied, kissing the top of my head.

I stopped walking and turned to face George completely and wrapped my arms around him lightly. My face was so close to his, I could feel his warm breath against my nose. I locked my eyes with his and took a deep breath, trying to keep my words coherent while I made the confession.

"You've changed my life, George. Every single part of it. It's incredible, isn't it? How one person has the power to make someone else's life a million times better," I whisper. "I wanted to thank you for every last thing you've done for me. I used to be an unconfident train wreck, and you've helped me become someone who doesn't care what others say; who doesn't have a panic attack every five minutes and who has found out who she is. You've given me the confidence to make new friends and I don't think you'll ever understand how much it all means to me."

I closed the minuscule gap between us and pressed my lips to his. An electric current coursed through my bloodstream like poison and I found myself craving more. I let the kiss linger for longer than I normally did in public, but unable to hold in the anticipation of what George would say to my spiel, I pulled away, breathing heavier than before.

"I also would never have been able to do that," I added as an afterthought.

"Zoe," George stammered, "I don't know what to say."

"Please tell me this is good speechless," I pleaded.

"This is amazing speechless."

"Thank God for that," I said, breathing out slowly.

"I'm just so happy that you're okay now. But all of this was on you, I didn't do anything. I just helped a little along the way, but you're the one who put the effort in, and I'm incredibly proud of you, my darling," George said finally.

Smiling at him in appreciation, I rested my head on his chest. We stayed there for a moment and I savoured the feeling of his fingers running through my hair. George leant away slightly and I lifted my face to look at him, eyebrows raised.

"Let's walk. We're nearly there," he said, looking ahead of us. I nodded and gladly let him drape his arm around my shoulder, holding me closer.

We walked for another five minutes or so; some in comfortable silence and some talking about everything and nothing at once. He led me off the main path towards one of the most beautiful trees I'd ever seen. It had pink blossoms everywhere, with only a few green leaves shining through. The branches spread out almost as wide as the tree was tall and it stood alone, the only thing surrounding it was an expanse of soft green grass.

He took me by the hand and pulled me closer to it, only stopping when we were just next to its colossal trunk. Sliding off his backpack, he unzipped it and pulled out a picnic blanket, carefully laying it on the grass. Sitting down, he gestured for me to do the same. Crossing my legs beneath me, I sat next to George, close enough to be touching, and used my thumb to rub his hand.

"I've got a full-blown picnic in there," he said, nodding his head towards his bag, "but I think some cuddles are needed first."

"Agreed."

George lay down on the blanket and held his arms out to let me lie with him. Happily, I fell into his arms, bringing them around me, holding onto them like they were my safety.

"I love you," I said after a moment, marvelling at the sheer amount of love I felt for him, and the emotion which exploded within me.

"I love you, too," George replied. "And I always will."

•••

And even if George didn't last forever, I'd still be eternally grateful for the fact I had him in my life and everything he did for me.

Because, besides, a year in technicolour is better than a lifetime in black and white monotone.

Author's Note

Firstly, thank you to all my beautiful and inspiring readers out there, because everyone is beautiful in their own way and we're all capable of doing amazing things. Thank you for choosing my book and I hope you enjoyed it.

I think it's important to say that in All The Things I Would Do, I've written it how I wish things were. Whereas in actual fact, it isn't that easy to just come out of yourself, as Zoe did. It would take a lot more work and time than I suggested, but that's because I wanted this story to be an ideal world, where you could simply decide you wanted to be better, and it was that easy. But I know from experience that it is not, however much we might wish it were.

One person probably doesn't have the power to change everything about yourself, and it will most likely take longer than six months to almost fully recover from anxiety and lack of confidence and all that Zoe was struggling with. But it's nice to pretend things can be that easy.

If you are struggling with anything similar, or not, to what Zoe was, then remember that you'll need to put in more time and effort and there will be ups and downs and there will be times when it seems impossible to go on, but I promise you, you can do it. You can get better and things will be alright in the end, even when it doesn't seem like it.

And for all those who hide: use this story as a sign that you don't have to hide in yourself or behind others. Be your own person and let others see who you are.

I wanted to show that it is worth the effort, even if Zoe didn't need to put this effort in, to become who you want to be and be able to live — really live. I promise you, it is worth it.

So, keep on fighting and remember: you are amazing and you don't have to hide. Never doubt it.

Amie

Acknowledgements

Firstly, thank you to my amazing family. Not because they helped me write this book — I never told them about it until after I'd finished it. But rather because they've always been there for me, supporting me and loving me through everything. Thank you for encouraging me to read and buying me all those books which sparked my interest in writing in the first place.

And while we're on books, thank you to the hundreds of authors I've read who inspired me to write my own book. I will be eternally grateful to whoever decided writing and reading books should be a thing and for allowing me to be a part of it.

Thank you to my sister, Emma Harrison Beesley, for accepting me as I am and for always looking out for me. You're the best big sister in the world.

Thank you to Grammarly, because God knows I wouldn't get through all the grammar on my own. And to spell check, because I am the queen of typos.

Thank you to my Wattpad followers, who read the first draft of this book and encouraged me to carry on writing, even when the story was cringe-worthy at this point. I'm grateful to all the lovely comments I received and it helped me carry on, especially when I was doubting my writing.

Thank you to Grace Thompson, who was always there for me when I needed someone to talk to and who'd always listen, even when I was rambling — which was often.

Finally, thank you to Diana Pando, who is an amazing friend even all the way over in Portugal. I can open my heart to you, and I've never felt so comfortable talking to someone; I can be completely myself with you. You make me smile and laugh and make me feel ok about myself. You believe in me even when I don't believe in myself and I love you for it.

Turn the page to read

Things I Wish She Would Do

A spin-off short story from George's perspective…

"You need to fix that bass of yours," I said disapprovingly to Dan. It'd been annoying me all practice and it made us all out of time and, frankly, it sounded like a dying cat.

"I know, mate. I'm working on it, alright?" Dan said, looking sheepish.

"I know, I was joking. Chill," I said to him, clapping my hand lightly on his shoulder before turning towards the door. "Bye, guys, see you later," I called over my shoulder to Tom and Bradley.

Shutting the door softly with a gentle click, I headed off towards tutor.

After only a couple of seconds, I caught sight of Zoe coming through the entrance to the school and walking the same way as I was. I slowed down and waited for her to catch up to me, knowing it wouldn't take long with the speed she was walking at. She wasn't late, but I didn't think she liked the corridors much — too likely for an encounter she wouldn't want to happen.

"Hey, Zoe," I said, trying to keep my voice as casual as possible. Thankfully, she slowed down enough so we could walk at a normal pace.

"Hi," Zoe said quietly. She said a lot of things quietly, like if she spoke too loudly someone might hear her.

"How was your weekend," I ventured weakly, desperate for something to talk about.

"Oh, it was fine. How was yours?" she said, a clear note of nerves in her voice. She smiled, though it barely reached her cheeks, let alone her eyes. But it created that sweet little dimple I rarely got to see. I didn't know if she talked like this to everyone, or just to some people who she wasn't comfortable with, but it sounded as though each word was laced with worry. Worry about what, I wasn't sure. Though I wished it weren't. I wished she could talk freely more often.

"It was good, thanks. I practised a new song on the guitar, but I can't seem to get it right." I tried for an easy-going answer, while also telling her something about myself, in a futile attempt to calm and reassure her, but I didn't think it worked.

Zoe smiled sweetly, looking up at me. I smiled back.

We came to my tutor room and I knew hers was the other end of the short corridor. I stopped just shy of the door and she got the hint and stopped too. "So, I'll catch you later?" I asked.

The fact that I'd surprised her was shown clearly on her face and she fumbled for a moment for something to say. "Um, yeah, sure," was all she managed.

I smiled again and started to head in, saying, "bye" over my shoulder at her. She mumbled "bye" back again, before heading off the hall to her own tutor room. I watched her walk away, with her delicate but fast steps. Gently pushing open the door, she disappeared from view. I went in then, too.

It made me sad, I thought, while I walked to my usual seat, seeing that Joe hadn't arrived yet, that she was so surprised that someone had, in a way, asked to see her again later. I got the feeling that that didn't happen to her very often. She'd blocked herself off from anyone willing to be friends with her so no one tried anymore – though I couldn't be sure many people noticed her much anyway. I couldn't imagine why someone would want to do that. Although, maybe I could. Maybe she was so scared of someone hurting her that she couldn't risk it, so she closed off her heart.

I hoped to change that all soon.

•••

I watched the seconds tick by on the obnoxiously loud clock on the wall in front of me. This was, by far, one of the most boring maths lessons I'd ever had, and it was clear I wasn't the only person thinking it. Yawns and absentminded tapping of pens surrounded me.

My eyes drifted over to where Zoe sat, a few seats to my right and in the row in front. As I watched her cower in her seat out of the corner of my eye, I suddenly wished she would sit up straighter and stop shying away from every living thing in sight. She deserved so much better; to feel better about herself and feel confident in her own body. But, even without her telling me the words, I knew how much she wished she were someone else. She deserved to know the truth: she didn't deserve this. No one did.

•••

There was something oddly satisfying about being a part of a huge stream of students and being the only one to turn away from the flow, I thought, as I did just that. My English classroom was the only room on the busiest corridor in the school and I nodded goodbye to Joe as he was swept away in the river. Pushing down on the handle, I stepped into the classroom and, without even thinking about it, I looked towards Zoe's seat.

She hadn't taken anything out of her bag yet, though it was on the table in front of her. She looked up at me and our eyes met as I fumbled with the door behind me, trying to push it closed while also attempting to calm my racing heart. It didn't matter that she almost always glanced away as soon as our eyes met or that she normally only ever gave small smiles, I still wanted to know everything about her and spend more time with her. It scared me how much I liked her.

I started walking to my seat, which was directly behind Zoe's, but I was still looking at her. I couldn't pull my eyes away. But then my step faltered. Because Zoe was smiling at me. Really smiling, lighting up her whole face in a way I'd only seen a couple of times. A smile pulled at my face and I imagined it mirrored hers, bright and wide in that uncontrollable way. I felt my heart flutter in my chest and the force of my feelings for her momentarily shocked me.

"Hey, how was band practice?" Zoe asked as I got to my seat, turning around to face me, her voice louder and surer than I'd ever heard her. A pleasant surprise flooded through me because she hardly ever spoke first or made a move to put herself out there, even a little bit. But I tried to hide my shock; it wasn't fair on her and I didn't want to embarrass her or make her feel self-conscious.

So I told her about how Dan's bass strap broke that morning and how we'd laughed when he was forced to sit down and how it was out of tune, distracting me the whole time. I laughed again at the memory and Zoe laughed too, the sound escaping out her mouth almost nervously, but I thought, distantly, that before today she never would have laughed at all.

I reluctantly stopped talking when Mr Reed called the class to attention. I was never very good at English, and I reluctantly flipped to the poem and accepted that I'd feel out of my depth for the next hour. At least, I thought, I could look at the back of Zoe's head and watch her scribble down her notes with an intense passion I could only wish for in a subject. But when Mr Reed asked a question, Zoe raised her hand. I was shocked, and it seemed apparent that everyone else in the class was too. We'd all been in the same class as Zoe for more than a year now and everyone had gotten used to her silent presence. Luckily, though, no one commented on it, for which I was grateful for Zoe's sake. Because it was clear she was really trying. Trying hard to focus on the question and ignore all the faces around her, maybe pretending she was writing but she was just speaking the words instead. I marvelled at her bravery and intelligence as she spoke because, even though I wasn't the best myself, I could appreciate good ideas from other people. And this was certainly a good idea.

The whole class seemed stunned into silence and it took the teacher a moment to compose himself and answer her: when he did, the pride was clear in his voice. Through the rest of the class, Zoe scribbled away in her anthology and answered questions with an obvious passion for the subject. It only made my feelings for her multiply.

When the lesson was over, I started packing up, feeling happy that I hadn't felt so utterly lost that lesson. Not because I suddenly understood English – far from it – but seeing Zoe like that made me forget about those things. Mr Reed came over as the students were filling out and I pretended to be looking at something in my bag as he talked to Zoe, congratulating her with a sincere smile and encouraging her to keep at it. I silently did the same.

Picking up her bag, Zoe gave me a smile over her shoulder before heading out of the classroom and I scrambled to do the same, hurrying out of the classroom after her and giving a rushed thanks to Mr Reed – who had a mischievous smile playing at his lips which I chose to ignore.

Zoe was a few steps in front of me, in the corridor which was partly empty for once, and I called out her name before I could talk myself out of it. Stopping walking, she spun around to face me, a smile on her face.

"Hey, I just wanted to say, well done for that. I know that must have taken some courage to speak up as you did. And, er, I'm proud of you," I said, hoping the nerves weren't audible in my voice. I was beaming at her, unable to do anything less at the sight of her. It was clear something had changed within Zoe. She held herself differently, like she wasn't trying to shy away from everything or avoid contact at all costs.

"Thank you, that means a lot," she said, smiling even wider. I wanted to hug her so badly then, It was almost as if a physical force was pushing me towards her and I had to resist it, knowing I'd only mess things up if I did that. I didn't know if she felt the same way about me – though I hoped she did – and I was reluctant to do anything that might ruin what we had already.

But, despite that, when we started walking to our next lesson, I pushed down my nerves and the doubt screaming at me to stop, and said, "I also wanted to ask, if you wouldn't mind, meeting me at lunch?"

She didn't say anything for a moment and I started to worry she'd say no and I'd have to act like it didn't bother me. I was just about to scramble for more to say when Zoe spoke. "Yeah, sure. Where do you want to meet?"

I relaxed, letting out a little breath I hadn't realised I was holding. I told her to meet me by the basketball courts at the beginning of lunch. She nodded enthusiastically and I relaxed more with the knowledge she really did want this. She looked as though she was about to say more, but we realised the class had already gone in so we sped up to slide into the classroom before the teacher closed the door. I wondered what she'd wanted to say.

She did smile, though, nodding, and I smiled back at her. Butterflies had already started flying around in my stomach at the thought of lunchtime alone with Zoe, finally more time with her. But even though I was nervous, I was happy at the idea and I hoped, with a strange need for it to come true, that this would be the start of something amazing.

Amie Collins is an English author, who has always had a passion for writing and creating and is currently living in the South of England. *All The Things I Would Do* is her debut novel. When she hasn't got her nose stuck in a book or writing, she enjoys listening to music, eating cake and drawing. She also enjoys playing with her dog and cat, although only one of them likes it (hint: her cat hates people).

Find out more about Amie Collins, *All The Things I Would Do* and more at:

www.amiecollins.co.uk

You can follow Amie on Instagram (@amiecollins) or read her blog (on her website).

Printed in Great Britain
by Amazon